WAR
Six
ENVY
NATIONAL BESTSELLING AUTHOR
T. STYLES

ARE YOU ON OUR EMAIL LIST?

SIGN UP ON OUR WEBSITE

www.thecartelpublications.com

OR TEXT THE WORD: CARTELBOOKS TO

22828

FOR PRIZES, CONTESTS, ETC.

Check out other titles by The Cartel Publications

Shyt List 1: Be Careful Who You Cross

Shyt List 2: Loose Cannon

Shyt List 3: And A Child Shall Leave Them

SHYT LIST 4: Children Of The Wronged

Shyt List 5: Smokin' Crazies The Finale'

Pitbulls in a Skirt 1

Pitbulls in a Skirt 2

Pitbulls In A Skirt 3: The Rise Of Lil C

Pitbulls In A Skirt 4: Killer Klan

Pitbulls In A Skirt 5: The Fall From Grace

Poison 1

Poison 2

Victoria's Secret

Hell Razor Honeys 1

Hell Razor honeys 2

Black and Ugly

Black and Ugly As Ever

Miss Wayne & The Queens of DC

Black and the Ugliest

A Hustler's Son

A Hustler's Son 2

The Face That Launched A Thousand Bullets

Year of the Crackmom

The Unusual Suspects

La Familia Divided

Raunchy

Raunchy 2: Mad's Love

Raunchy 3: Jayden's Passion

Mad Maxxx: Children of The Catacombs (Extra Raunchy)

Kali: Raunchy Relived: The Miller Family

Reversed

Quita's DayScare Center

Quita's DayScare Center 2

DEAD HEADS

DRUNK & HOT GIRLS

PRETTY KINGS

PRETTY KINGS 2: SCARLETT'S FEVER

PRETTY KINGS 3: DENIM'S BLUES

PRETTY KINGS 4: RACE'S RAGE

HERSBAND MATERIAL

UPSCALE KITTENS

WAKE & BAKE BOYS

YOUNG & DUMB

YOUNG & DUMB: VYCE'S GETBACK

TRANNY 911

TRANNY 911: DIXIE'S RISE

FIRST COMES LOVE, THEN COMES MURDER

LUXURY TAX

THE LYING KING

CRAZY KIND OF LOVE

SILENCE OF THE NINE

SILENCE OF THE NINE II: LET THERE BE BLOOD

SILENCE OF THE NINE III

PRISON THRONE

GOON

HOETIC JUSTICE

AND THEY CALL ME GOD

THE UNGRATEFUL BASTARDS

LIPSTICK DOM

A SCHOOL OF DOLLS

SKEEZERS

SKEEZERS 2

YOU KISSED ME NOW I OWN YOU

NEFARIOUS

REDBONE 3: THE RISE OF THE FOLD

THE FOLD

CLOWN NIGGAS

THE ONE YOU SHOULDN'T TRUST

COLD AS ICE

THE WHORE THE WIND BLEW MY WAY

SHE BRINGS THE WORST KIND

THE HOUSE THAT CRACK BUILT

THE HOUSE THAT CRACK BUILT 2: RUSSO & AMINA

THE HOUSE THAT CRACK BUILT 3: REGGIE & TAMIKA

THE HOUSE THAT CRACK BUILT 4: REGGIE & AMINA

LEVEL UP

VILLAINS: IT'S SAVAGE SEASON

GAY FOR MY BAE

WAR

WAR 2

WAR 3

WAR 4

WAR 5

WAR 6

THE END. HOW TO WRITE A BESTSELLING NOVEL IN 30 DAYS

WWW.THECARTELPUBLICATIONS.COM

WAR 6

ENVY

By

T. STYLES

PUBLISHER'S NOTE:
This book is a work of fiction. Names, characters, businesses,
Organizations, places, events and incidents are the product of the
Author's imagination or are used fictionally. Any resemblance of
Actual persons, living or dead, events, or locales are entirely coincidental.

Library of Congress Control Number: 2020901432

ISBN 10: 1948373114

ISBN 13: 978-1948373111

Cover Design: Book Slut Girl

First Edition
Printed in the United States of America

What Up Fam,

I hope ya'll having a good 2020 so far! Can't even believe it's the end of January already. Before we know it, it'll be Memorial Day. As I'm writing this letter the news broke about the passing of Kobe Bryant and his daughter Gianna (along with seven others) in a helicopter crash. I'm devastated by this. It seems unreal but it serves as a reminder that we are not here forever. Make sure you make the best of each and every day 'cuz they go by quick. And most importantly, don't forget selfcare. If you not good, you can't make sure your loved ones are good. Also, stop to have fun. Laugh, sing, dance and love like its your last!

Whew…Now…The War series…This has to absolutely be T. Styles' BEST book series to date! I know I'm biased, and I know I've said this before about RAUNCHY, SILENCE OF THE NINE, SHYT LIST and many more, but, I swear, this series pulls me in more and more with each addition! I LOVE these fuckin' characters and find myself thinking about them way after the book closes. That's how vicious her pen game is! And WAR 6 stands right up to the series and owes me nothing!! You in for another great read!!

With that being said, keeping in line with tradition, we want to give respect to a vet or new trailblazer paving the way. In this novel, we would like to recognize:

LAMAR JACKSON

Lamar Demeatrice Jackson is my QB of the Baltimore Ravens! He was selected as the 32nd Pick in the first round of the 2018 NFL Draft to the Ravens and was quoted as saying, "They gonna get a SUPERBOWL out of me. Believe that." That was a strong statement from someone who was only 21 and I wasn't sure I was convinced but it didn't take long to see that this amazing guy was serious and ready to work. Fast forward to this season, Lamar and the Ravens weren't able to make it to the SB sadly but did defend their AFC North crown and completed the regular season at 14-2! Now, Lamar, who just won the 2020 Pro Bowl Offensive MVP, is on the brink of becoming the league's MVP. All at the age of 23 and we as RAVENS fanatics are very excited about his future here! I see nothing but greatness in this young bull! We at The Cartel Publications LOVE him are EXTREMELY proud of him!

Aight, I'm done fan-doming. Dive in!

God Bless!

Charisse "C. Wash" Washington

Vice President

The Cartel Publications

www.thecartelpublications.com

www.facebook.com/publishercwash

Instagram: publishercwash

www.twitter.com/cartelbooks

www.facebook.com/cartelpublications

Follow us on Instagram: Cartelpublications

#CartelPublications

#UrbanFiction

#PrayForCece

#LamarJackson

#RIPKobe&GiGi

#War6

PREVIOUSLY ON WAR 5

The midwives fussed around Jersey as she lied in a bed within the maternity room Banks had set up for her on her estate. He was proud as he looked down at the woman who had just given birth to his twin boys which they named Ace and Walid.

They were his flesh and blood.

When they were done cleaning her and the babies, Banks sat on the side of the bed and looked down at the nude infants she nestled against her body. He pulled the covers up enough to give all three warmth.

Smiling proudly, he wiped her hair behind her ear and looked down at her beautiful face. "You, you actually did it."

"What?" She said, already knowing the answer but loving to hear the words.

The babies cooed lightly.

"You gave birth to twins."

"Your sons." She emphasized. "Of your flesh and blood."

He nodded, more proudly.

When Jersey first said she wanted to give him babies, he thought she was lying. After all, she would have to go through the invasive process of having Banks' eggs implanted with a sperm donor and deposited into her body. The same thing Bet did with Minnie.

Originally the procedure netted in quintuplets, but he later had three removed to allow for an easier pregnancy. It was an invasive procedure, but she was game, in the name of love.

"I've never been happier." He admitted.

"And I'm so pleased I could do this for you, Banks." She looked up at him and smiled.

"I'm happy for you too."

When Banks heard another voice in the room, chills ran down his spine when he turned around to see Mason hanging in the doorway.

Smiling.

Trying to get him away from the love of his life and his twins he quickly rose and said, "Let's talk out there."

"Nah," he walked deeper into the room. "We talking right here."

It was at that time Banks could see the five men in the hallway, holding the midwives and two of his bodyguards at gunpoint.

As if they knew what was coming, both babies suddenly wept.

"Mason, please, please don't," Jersey whispered as tears trailed her cheek and fell on her babies faces.

"Don't do what? Allow you to live in peace and harmony with my best fucking friend? You gave this nigga babies!" He roared. "It's one thing to fuck her," he said looking at Banks. "But, ya'll niggas crossed the line." He put his hands on his chest. "I mean, is it just me or are ya'll actually in LOVE?!" Tears rolled down his cheeks.

"Mason, it's not like you didn't—."

"I'M NOT TRYING TO HEAR THAT SHIT ABOUT ME FUCKING BET NO MORE!" He said, cutting Jersey off. "THE GUILT TRIP SHIT IS DEAD! IT WAS DONE WHEN IT WAS DONE!" He took a deep breath. "But you two, you two took it too far. You fell in love."

She looked at Banks who shuffled a few steps.

"What you want, Mason? Anything you want and it's done." Banks wasn't a begging man. But he would get on his knees if he thought it was worth it. Besides, he just met his sons and already he was deeply in love with them. And he would do what was necessary to protect their newborn lives.

"I want to tell you something that's very important." Mason smiled. "Something you may wanna know."

Banks glared, not trusting his disposition or motives. "What?"

"I found out early on about all this baby making shit. I just wanted, I just wanted you to tell me

yourself, nigga. That last time you visited me in the institution." Mason continued, trembling with rage. "You owed me more but you, you couldn't do it. And I remember thinking, I can't believe my guy is this foul."

Jersey said, "Mason, can we talk about—"

"You don't say shit else to me," he responded, aiming his barrel at Jersey's head. "I'm done with yo ho ass!"

Banks stepped in front of the gun, blocking the barrel's path.

Unable to kill his man, Mason lowered it and looked down. "I knew before she did the procedure. Had her followed when she left the house."

"How?" Banks asked.

"Derrick told me." He walked away. "So I, so I let her do it. I let her have your babies. But you need to know something, Banks. Those kids, those boys, are ours."

Banks frowned and stepped back. "What...what...you...what you talking about?"

"I don't need to tell you that with money you can do anything. So, it was easy to have my sperm mixed with your eggs for this procedure." He smiled like a mad man and walked over to Jersey. Looking down at their twins he said, "I mean, look what we built. They're perfect."

Jersey's eyes widened as she stared down at the babies, trying to find one hint of it being true. And there, on Ace's hand, was a tiny birthmark that Howard also had on his little finger. And she knew it was all facts.

Banks backed into the wall and slid down.

"We created a new generation of Lou's and Wales'." He walked over to Banks and stood over top of him. "And it's perfect. Don't you see, Banks? Ain't no getting rid of me. Ain't no getting rid of us now."

"I...I can't believe...you...did this." Banks whispered.

"What God has joined together let no man tear apart, without first catching a bullet." Mason smiled. "We joined together now. Which brings me to my next question. You have one decision to make. Just one." He put his hand over his heart.

Banks' eyes were glassed over and red, having been exposed to his betrayal of the highest order. Mason had been wanting them to be combined all his life, and finally he created a situation where they had children together.

Two beautiful twin boys.

"What...what do you want?" Banks glared.

"You have to choose. Do you want our sons or Jersey's life?" He stooped down. "Because you can't have both. So, tell me my love, what's it gonna be?"

CHAPTER ONE

The full moon was embedded inside the seams of a midnight blue sky. As if it were judging and glaring down at Mason as he sat on the plantation style porch on Jersey's estate, purchased for her by his best friend Banks.

One of his soldiers hung close by on the ready, in case Banks somehow orchestrated a hit on his life from the inside.

As an owl hooted in the distance, he was in his own thoughts which were as thick as maple syrup. Many things needed to be considered in the moment. Things that would yet again change the course of his relationship with Banks.

Of that he was certain.

Afterall, he was forcing Banks to make a decision, albeit an impossible one, to choose between the lives of Jersey and their twin sons. To make sure they didn't flee into the night, he left his soldiers in her room and had given him until the end of the hour.

His demand was callous and vicious.

And he didn't give a fuck.

When the door opened, Mason reached for his hammer until he saw one of his soldiers with Tobias at his side. “Sorry, boss. He wanted to speak with you. He’s not armed. We checked.”

Mason nodded and allowed Tobias to walk outside, after all, he was Bolero’s son.

Taking a deep breath, Tobias sat next to him and for a moment they both looked at the sparkling sky. Crickets chirped in song, and in the distance a wolf howled.

“Do you ever think God is ashamed of what we’ve become?” Tobias asked, his Latin accent thick but precise.

Mason bit the inside of his lip. “I don’t allow myself to think of those things. It won’t serve me much anyway.”

He nodded. “I don’t either. Until I experience a night like this where you’re forced to come to terms with death.”

Mason shuffled a little. He felt an order of begging coming along in Banks’ name. “What you want, nigga? Huh? Get to the fucking point.”

“I really don’t want anything.”

“Everybody wants something.” He glared harder. “I don’t see why you should be any different.”

Tobias took a deep breath. He didn’t *really* know the man and yet he would not be who he was becoming if he bit his tongue. “You’re wrong on what you’re about to do, sir. In most ways.”

Mason rose quickly and removed his gun pressing it against the back of Tobias' head. One bad move and things could change for them both. After all, Tobias was the plug's son, even if their relationship was strained.

Would it really serve him to take his life?

Still, Mason didn't know what he was expecting to hear but it certainly wasn't that he was to blame. The way Mason saw the matter, he was the victim. He was the one who trusted his best friend only for him to violate him and the most horrendous way.

Those were the facts and they were hard and real.

"Give me one good reason why I shouldn't kill you right now?" Mason asked through clenched teeth.

"You shouldn't because I come in the name of the truth." Tobias' gaze remained on the horizon. "You don't want to kill Banks. You don't want to kill Jersey or the kids either."

"I never said I wanted to kill Banks."

"If you kill that woman, or the twins, that's exactly what you'll be doing."

"You overstepping your boundaries."

"You may be right. But I'm a man. And if it's my lot in life to die because I choose to speak the truth," a deeper breath, "then squeeze the trigger."

Mason couldn't understand but for some reason he felt inclined to at least hear the man out. Perhaps it was his braveness. So, he tucked his weapon in his waistline and reclaimed his seat, although it was a few feet away from Tobias.

"Okay, I'm listening. Why am I wrong when they both violated my trust?"

Tobias looked at him. "I don't have to remind you that I was there. On the island. After you were caught having sex with Banks' wife. I saw the disappointment on his face. You ripped him up in a way that stays with you long after it's done. Is this revenge?" He shrugged. "Maybe. But I don't think he knows. I believe he believes he's in love with her."

Mason's jaw twitched. "I'm sick of people bringing up the same thing over and over. As if I don't know what happened. As if, as if I don't sleep with that shit every fucking night. But this hits different." He pointed at the door. "He fell in love with my wife. And she fell in love with him. I'm the one who's destroyed and they...and they don't give a fuck. Even now."

He looked down; fists clenched in knots so tight they paused the blood from circulating through his hands.

Tobias nodded. "I happen to agree with you. They took things to a disrespectful level."

Hearing the affirmation for some reason gave Mason immediate peace. Throughout this journey there was always someone waiting in the dark spaces to tell him he was the villain. To tell him how badly he hurt others. And although most were right, it still stung. Like a wound that refused to heal.

"If I'm so right, if that's what you really believe, why do I get the impression you trying to stop me from what I need to do?"

"You lost two sons, sir. I know the feeling of losing loved ones." A deeper breath tickled his throat as he reminisced about Skull Island. "I lost two sisters. It hurts to this day."

Mason shifted a little since his stupid behavior was the cause of one of his sister's demise.

"And still the one thing I would never be able to deal with is the loss of my mother. There is no greater wound. I've seen Minnesota, Joey and Spacey's faces at the Wales estate. They try to hide the pain, but it has become a part of their story. And so, there is no escape."

"Get to the point."

"You have one son left, sir."

"Two...I have two sons left." Mason glared referring to Howard.

"I'm sorry, you're right." Tobias corrected himself. "Think about what it would do to them if you took their mother's life. A man growing up without a father is confused. A man growing up without a mother becomes a monster."

"So, I'm supposed to let them run away together? In my face? With, with my twins? Is that what you saying?"

"Believe it or not I'm not here to judge. I'm not here to get you to make any decision either. I just want you not to...I just want you not to do anything tonight. Let her breast-feed her babies. Let her give them the love they need in the early days of their lives. And then if you decide to kill her, if that's the decision that Banks makes when it is time to choose, then at least you know you've given the matter honest thought."

His words had landed but Mason wasn't in the mercy mood. He wanted revenge ripped away in flesh and rested at his feet.

"My body wants blood. My body wants retaliation."

"I understand, sir. But have you asked your heart?"

CHAPTER TWO

The moment was ominous, and he knew it but still Banks tried his best to drag out every second, every minute of the time he was spending with Jersey and their sons.

As he looked down at her cradling them both, he tried to hold himself together. He knew Mason enough to realize that when he made a threat regardless of how reckless, he would see his viciousness through.

Nervously, Gina, the nanny, walked up to Jersey. She was an older white woman wearing a gray wig that sat too far to the left. But it was obvious she knew babies. "Did you need anything else, Mrs. Louisville?"

"Mrs. Wales." Banks corrected her, despite them not being married. "Call her Mrs. Wales."

The woman's eyes widened. "Sir, I'm so sorry. I didn't mean anything by it. I just..."

She looked down and he immediately felt bad. His rage was misdirected at best. "It's no problem," he said.

She nodded in relief. "I'll prepare the bottles over there." She replied, before walking to the other side of the room to the baby bar.

When she walked away Jersey said, "I'm so sorry, Banks. About Mason and...and all of this. I didn't know, I didn't know he would go this far." Tears streamed down her cheeks. "I didn't know he would try to hold on to me so tightly. It's not like when we were together that he showed me love."

Banks wiped her hair out of her face and tucked it behind her ear. "It's never about what you think it is with him."

"But your life was fine before today."

"Things been rough at home, Jersey. It hadn't been sweet."

"What you mean?"

"Losing Bet made shit harder on the kids. All of 'em home now, even Joey. And they been asking questions on how she died. And I ain't got the answers to none of that shit. So, it's been fucking with my mind. Sometimes...sometimes I wish I could start all over, with just you and the boys."

"Don't say that."

"I already did."

Gina walked back over and handed Jersey the bottles.

"Thank you." Jersey replied.

Banks pulled up a chair and took Ace and a bottle. The moment the infant was in his arms, his little body melted into his like butter. The baby's scent. His little feet. He loved them so much it was hard to fathom being without them.

"Mason's rage is about me not being happy without him. That's what it's always been about. I mean look at what's happening. He actually, he actually…used his own sperm to…to…"

He couldn't say the words.

He couldn't say out loud that Mason overstepped his boundaries so far as to mix his sperm with his eggs. Single handedly fucking up the vision he had for his new life with Jersey. Because it was crystal, that by doing so, Mason had essentially become the twins' father, which made Banks their mother.

And Banks hated him for fucking with his identity as a man.

At the same time, he blamed himself for not seeing this move coming. After all, the seasons may have changed, people may have died, but one thing remained consistent. Mason's unrelenting desire to embed himself into Banks' life from here until eternity.

Banks lived by the motto that when people show you who they are, you should believe them. So, hadn't Mason always been crystal on his intentions?

And then there were the months leading up to the day. Banks was in love and so excited about the arrival of his children that he didn't notice the mental absence of his best friend.

But there were *signs.*

Mason was too reserved and laid back. But Banks assumed his being in the mental hospital after attempting to take his life after losing Patterson, had somehow miraculously changed him from the sinister man he was born to be.

He was wrong.

And it was this comfort that allowed him to take his eyes off of Mason Louisville. A move that would haunt him for the rest of his life.

"I've always loved Mason as a brother but this act...this level of disrespect, it destroyed the last place in my heart that I—."

She touched his hand. "I know. And I feel so stupid. I've been in regular contact with Derrick and he never let on that he told his father about us being together. Or that he had me followed. And I know he didn't know that I was pregnant. We were very careful. So why did he lie on his son?"

"I'm not sure. But Derrick, he, he violated with this move."

"He chose his father over me. He knew what kind of man he was and he still, he still put me in danger." Her body trembled as she continued. "I don't want to hate my son. I truly don't but this...this hurts like cold steel into my heart."

Mason's arrival was the worst thing that could have happened for their love story. For a brief moment, Banks imagined that for once in his life he would have happily ever after. And at the same time did he believe he deserved a storybook ending? He was a hustler. And hustlers lived by two codes.

Money and death.

Love was never on the agenda. Because love was fleeting and always in lieu of being, doing or having paper. People said you couldn't buy love. But Banks Wales believed those who uttered those ridiculous words weren't rich enough.

"I take responsibility for what happened to us." His voice was firm and laced with regret. "If I had it to do over, I wouldn't put you through this. I would've been smarter and—"

"I don't want you to talk like that again."

"Why?"

"I know what you're about to say, Banks and I'll have no more of that." She shook her head slowly as tears fell. "If this is our last moment, I want it selfishly apart from Mason."

He sat back and held his baby a little tighter.

She looked down at Walid. "We would have always ended up here some kind of way."

"We didn't have to go with how we felt. We could have resisted."

"There was no turning back for me. The moment I saw your eyes open on me, like really open, I was done. Yes, Mason is forcing you to, you to make a decision that I know is hard to decide." Tears crept slowly. "But I'm glad we had us, Banks. For the first time I feel alive. More alive than ever."

He did too.

"And I remember," she wiped her tears away and took a deep breath. "...boarding your plane before me and my family went to Wales island. When we brought Minnesota back to you. For some reason, the moment I saw your face I had an unexplainable sense of relief that stayed with me like a warm sweater on a cool night." She smiled, as her mind recalled the day. "I had no idea that my peace came from seeing you again."

"My plans were to kill you. We were at war."

"Aren't we always?"

He nodded, upon hearing the truth.

She kissed her baby's forehead. "War or not, you and I were always in sync. We always knew how to speak to one another. And if death becomes of this relationship then to me it's worth it." She put the bottle on the bed.

He really hoped she meant it because his decision was made.

There was no way on God's green earth that he could see a scenario where he spared her life over his twins. Just when he was about to let her know she would be dead within the hour, Mason walked through the door covered by four men.

Slowly, he moved ahead of his soldiers and stood in the middle of the floor. His eyes were red like cherries. It was not due to crying. He hadn't shed another tear.

It was pure rage.

"You don't need to make a decision tonight," he said, barely able to look at Banks' face due to the pain of his betrayal.

Banks exhaled and sat the bottle on the floor. It wasn't until that moment he realized he had been holding his breath.

"Oh my God, thank you!" Jersey yelled, causing her babies to rouse and cry. "Thank you so much."

He glared at her, wanting desperately to feel the soft tissue of her throat under his fingertips. "I'm not doing this for you, bitch!"

"Mason, hold fast." Banks frowned, not feeling the disrespect. "She didn't mean anything by—."

"Nah, nigga, you hold fast!" He snapped, while also reconsidering his grace. The fact that they didn't understand he had the right to take lives that night made him ill. "I'm doing this for Derrick and Howard. And I'm doing this for our sons." He said pointing to the babies.

Banks couldn't think about him mentioning Howard because the moment he heard *'our sons'* he felt a new level of rage. It was as if all of his life the only hate he experienced reached from floor one to thirteen. But now hearing Mason refer to his twin sons as his too, he realized there was a new level. Level ninety-nine and it took everything in his power to prevent rising and destroying him where he stood.

It was Ace's soft whines that brought him back to the moment and the fact that with the men Mason had waiting in the hallway, he was outnumbered. Which meant Banks had zero control.

Banks sat back in his chair, and softly rocked his baby. His calm manner allowed his son to fall back to sleep. "What now?" Banks glared.

"The boys will stay here six days out of the week. So that Jersey can breast feed them. You can take them on the seventh day."

With the rules etched like the Ten Commandments in stone, Banks wanted to commit murder. "These aren't your sons."

"I'm not done."

Banks gritted his teeth.

"Jersey will stay in my possession until I figure out what I'll do to her. In case you act slick, and don't bring the boys back. On the other days of the week you don't have the twins, you can come here to visit them. But my people will remain, always watching Jersey. Don't get her killed doing something stupid."

Banks' left leg shook. "What else?"

"I'll let you know, baby mama." He winked at Banks and exited the room, while being sure to leave his men behind.

Tobias hung in the doorway.

Derrick's drinking reached a new high. After losing Arlyndo, later Patterson and possibly Howard, his temper which at one point was under control, had gotten out of hand.

And then there was his girlfriend, Shay Wales.

Why couldn't she obey?

Earlier that morning he tried to make love, but she was talking to some new friends at the hair salon on the phone and wasn't in the mood to fuck.

"Not right now," she said, as she shoved him away with a flat palm. "Maybe later." She returned to her conversation, which included laughing with her friends about him begging for pussy.

She was flexing hard.

His issue with her in that moment was simple. Their arrangement was supposed to be reciprocated on both sides. When he wanted sex, she promised to oblige. And in return he would offer her what she desired.

A Louisville man on her arm.

But it seemed like since they moved in together, she wasn't willing to play the role anymore.

What was it with women who didn't seem to know their place? He thought.

It wasn't like they couldn't have the world simply because of the pussy situated between their legs. In his opinion women possessed an unfair advantage in the ability to make a man beg.

That went for his mother too.

He had been thinking about her a lot. Yes, he felt disloyal for telling his father about her relationship with Banks. But in his mind, she was due everything that was coming her way, short of murder. And at the same time what would've happened if his father killed her?

How did he even know she was still alive?

Without Arlyndo, Patterson and not knowing where Howard was located, the Louisville clan would be demolished.

The breakdown of his family and his recent sense of loneliness was the main reason he tried to hold onto his relationship with Mason. It was to the point of pushiness.

Lately whenever Mason went somewhere Derrick was riding shotgun. Whether it be taking a drive to New York to see their cousins, or going to the casino to rock the tables, he simply wanted to remain in his presence.

Still in his bedroom, he was playing a video game and deciding on whether or not to let his rage against Shay go when she walked inside the room. Wearing a T-shirt with no bra and shorts that tucked into her ass and pussy, he hated himself for wanting her more.

She sat on the edge of the bed. Legs open just to be nasty. "I know you still not mad, nigga. Just 'cause I didn't give you none."

He knew what she was trying to do. Bait him. And he was determined not to let her have more control. Since she didn't want to put out, he figured he could get it from somewhere else later on that night. So, he continued to play the game ignoring her altogether.

She glared. “I know you hear me talking to you! Why you still got an attitude?”

He pushed the buttons harder on the controller as his limbs moved along with the game. “I don’t have an attitude. You made your decision.” He shrugged. “I guess I gotta deal with it. Although I will be getting my dick sucked by you or somebody later.”

Something had to give because he was rock hard.

“I hate when you act goofy. If something on your mind, speak it. I am your girlfriend.”

“Like I said, I don’t feel like talking right now.”

All of his attention appeared to remain on the game. But he was in auto drive. He wasn’t even thinking about his moves. He played so many times that it was effortless. In the moment it was all about ignoring her and getting his mind off of life.

Embarrassed, she stood up and hung in the doorway, glaring his way.

He could feel her rage and thought it was cute when she got mad. And at the same time, he knew if she got too heated things could get violent. After all it’s not like she hadn’t killed before.

He was just about to put the game down when she smacked him on the side of the face. So hard it caused his temples to rock.

Livid, he tossed the game controller and rushed up to her, bare feet slapping against the floor.

Grabbing her by the shoulders, he shook her hard, like a dusty rug. "What the fuck is wrong with you?"

She smiled. "You think I'm a game, so I had to show you I'm not."

He shoved her into the wall and pointed a stiff finger in her face. "Bitch, I could've killed you!"

"Do it!" She shrugged. "If you gonna stay mad at me I don't care no more."

She wanted to fight so he let her go.

Besides, there was no use in talking to crazy. "That jealous shit you got going on is going to give you an infection. You better watch how you living."

"You started this not me."

"Why? Because I asked for some pussy?"

"I'm your girlfriend, not your slave. And if I have to teach you how to treat me that's exactly what I'm gonna do."

He walked closer. "Let me tell you something. If I don't get pussy, whenever I ask, how I ask, you gonna get the fuck up out my house. I ain't even gonna play these games with you no more. I'm just gonna grab you by your hair and throw you out on the streets."

"I'm a Wales. I'll never be homeless."

"Then it shouldn't be a problem." He paused. "So, what you gonna do?"

After staring him down for a while, she pushed him on the bed and got on top of him. Removing his dick, which always thickened when they fought, she eased him into her slick pussy as a smile spread over her face. "With your mean ass."

CHAPTER THREE

The rain came down with vengeance over the Wales estate.

Minnesota sat in her room staring out the window as she tried to think about her life. So much happened over the years, including the new changes to her body. She filled out in places she hadn't thought of and her hips curved in preparation for childbirth, if she so desired.

But what kept her up at night or crying into her pillow was her circumstances.

First Harris was murdered and then her mother. It appeared to be a killing each year.

When would it all stop?

She even felt a type of way over the loss of her last boyfriend Arlyndo Louisville. Sure, he was a monster. Sure, she knew the horror he was capable of, but it didn't make her miss him any less.

People often said you become stronger the more you struggled, and she believed it was true.

Still, she preferred if the dark cloud over her family would go away.

In a need of a hobby, recently she had taken up journaling. Scribbled on the pages were her thoughts of Harris and her mother and all the times she used to fight with them over the silliest of things. In hindsight, it was apparent how stupid it was to waste time on things that didn't matter.

Again, when would it all stop?

And then there was Banks. Why was he being so secretive? What was going on in his life that he assumed she couldn't handle? Was it the murder of her mother?

Because there were *many* questions.

As of the day all she knew was for some reason Howard was responsible, but he didn't tell her, Spacey or Joey why.

The only bright side of it all was the eighteenth birthday party Banks was throwing for her in September. She went over every detail and although he normally didn't allow people in their home, for her he promised to be lenient, provided the celebration was heavily armed with security.

She was just about to hit the shower to run the rainy streets when Tobias walked into her room. Admiring her beauty, he leaned against the doorframe and for a second she couldn't get over how handsome he was. His perfect looks were the reason she gave him such a hard time. A man that fine let the world know the moment he stepped through the door without saying word one.

The other reason she resented him was simple. She was underage, and he was intent on respecting her youth.

Sure, she would be a woman that year, but she hated him for making her wait. Horny as fuck, she did all she could to get his attention. Walking around the mansion in revealing clothing. Asking him for small favors around the house, wrapped in nothing but a towel and shea butter.

Still, nothing mattered.

Tobias had always been serious about his stance when it came to protecting her innocence. He didn't want to have sex. He didn't even want them thinking about it until she was a woman.

And although it was respectful on his part, she would've preferred a full-blown rape rather than being ignored.

Doing a horrible job of being unbothered, she grabbed her hair and caressed it into a bun that sat on top of her head. "What you want?"

"I wanted to say hi."

That accent. It simply drove her wild. "Well say hi and get the fuck outta my face."

He said, "Hola, Minnesota, mi Amor."

Her heart skipped a beat and her bun flopped in her face. "Tobias, I don't have time for this." She whipped her hair away.

"What did I ever do to you?" He asked seriously. "To deserve this kind of behavior? My worst crime was respecting you."

"Are you respecting my father's wishes or mine? Because I made clear what I want, and you refused me."

He shook his head. "Does it matter?"

She rolled her eyes. Sure, he was respectful, but he wasn't bold or dangerous enough and she needed a passionate man. Maybe it was the little girl in her that still desired a wild boy.

"I'm getting ready to get in the shower." She wrapped the belt around her robe tighter. "And that wasn't an invitation." A deep breath. "It's not like you would've taken me up on my offer if it was anyway."

"You'll be eighteen soon, Minnesota."

"And that'll be too late. What we have has an expiration date."

"Meaning?"

"I'm not interested in you any longer, Tobias."

He smiled because he didn't believe her. "Anyway, you have company."

She frowned. "Who?"

"Why don't you go see for yourself."

After getting dressed, holding an umbrella she went outdoors, surprised to see Myrio standing on the other side of the gate surrounding the property in a red designer raincoat. Since he was unable to enter the Wales land, she took the long walk to meet him instead, holding a small gold box in her hand. Even though she exited the gate, there were soldiers with AK's able to shoot Myrio where he stood if she was in distress.

What she also noticed was the silver Aston Martin sitting next to him with a drenched red bow on the top.

A gift?

Maybe.

She couldn't help but smile.

"What you doing here?" She asked putting her hand on her hip.

"You wouldn't answer my last text message." He looked at the small box. "And what you got in your hand?"

"None of your business."

He grinned.

"I thought I told you not to call me."

"That was yesterday. Besides, I came over to give you an early birthday present. That should be good for an exception."

"My birthday months away."

"It's yours anyway."

She looked at the car and it was magnificent. "I can buy my own car."

"You can but you didn't." He paused and nodded at the vehicle. "Come on, get in with me. Let's see how it fits."

Interested, she quickly slid into the vehicle. Again, the soldiers were aiming in the event something went wrong.

But as of the moment all was well.

Once inside, she was enamored by the design as she sat in the driver's seat. The new car smell was intoxicating. It was a beautiful vehicle with yam colored interior, and she was thoroughly impressed.

He threw the hood to his coat back, exposing his handsome face. "Like it?"

Thunder ripped through the sky. Placing the box on her lap she glanced him over as she took in his features. Neat haircut kept low. Designer blue jeans, a white t-shirt and a red Gucci windbreaker. She was definitely loving his style. In a lot of ways, he reminded her of Arlyndo, and she wondered if that was good or bad.

"I thought I told you to leave me alone. And what do you do? Come over with a new car."

"And I thought I told you when you said you were busy, that you were my woman and I'll see you whenever I desire."

She forced back a smile. He was bolder than Tobias. "I haven't agreed."

"That's just a technicality. Within time, I'll have you eating out of my hands."

"Things are complicated."

"I know. You feeling Bolero's son."

She frowned. "How do you know about him? I never told you that."

"Are you serious? It's on front street news." He looked toward the estate.

Minnesota glanced across the way and sure enough Tobias was standing in the doorway watching.

She felt bad for him.

Not because she'd done anything wrong by being with Myrio. After all they were not together. But she felt foul because she knew she was falling for another man.

Over it all, she sat back and ran her fingers over the steering wheel. "I don't want this car."

"Yeah you do."

"You gonna force me to take it?"

"Nah. Why do things with force when you can do them with ease?" He winked. "The car is yours. Do what you want with it."

He flopped on his hood and rushed out of the vehicle.

Minnesota grabbed her umbrella and the box and rushed out. Fumbling with the umbrella, he ran up to her and opened it, holding it over her head to protect her from the rain.

"Thank you." She smiled. "Here." She extended the box.

He took it from her hand. "What is it?"

"Find out."

She took the umbrella and he opened the box, revealing a customized Gucci watch. "What's this?" He asked.

"The invitation to my party in September. It's awhile out but you have to wear it to get inside. It'll be here."

He smiled. "Your father bought two thousand-dollar watches as an invitation for your party?"

She shrugged.

"Dope. Maybe you can come scoop me up." He smiled, winked and walked away.

With a black umbrella over his head, Tobias arrived at the Louisville mansion with a duffel bag in hand. The moment he knocked on the door, he was immediately greeted by Derrick. "Why Banks didn't come his self? He doesn't wanna see us no more? I mean he was fucking my mother, right?"

"You have to talk to Banks about that." He looked past him into the house. "Is your father here?" He raised the bag. "I think he'll want to see me."

He nodded and thunder clapped the sky. "Come inside."

Tobias dropped the umbrella and followed Derrick toward Mason's office. It wasn't as fly as Banks', but it did have flair. Movie posters in frames. Rap icons like Biggie, Jay Z and the like also around. It fit his personality greatly.

"I have your money."

Mason nodded. "Have a seat."

He complied.

"Give me the bag."

Tobias handed it to him. "It's all there."

Mason sighed, unzipped it open and scanned the contents quickly. He had never known Banks to cheat him and he doubt he'd start now. "Thanks. Now get out." He focused on the property forms on his desk.

Instead of leaving, Tobias hung back a little and Mason raised his eyes from the documents in irritation. "What you still doing here?"

"I have to talk to you about something. Actually, I don't know who to talk to about anything to be honest. I know we aren't friends but—"

"I don't have time for this."

"And I don't have anybody else. Please, Mason. Just five minutes of your time. Not a second more."

Mason sat deeper in his chair and sighed. With his fingers folded on the agreements he said, "Make it quick."

"Minnesota isn't...what do you say... feeling me."

"Feeling you huh? Even talking like niggas now and everything."

"Some man has been coming by asking about her. And I fear the fact that I'm not a violent guy may work against me. Don't get me wrong, I used to be that way but losing sisters changed something inside of me."

Mason didn't agree with being passive, but he let him speak. "Don't lose the part of you that gives you edge."

"I desire nothing more than peace. And I don't think she wants that."

"It's not that she doesn't want peace. You're dealing with a rich woman. Even worse, she was born rich. And rich women favor dangerous men. It excites the boredom out of their lives."

"So, what do I do? To become what she needs me to be?"

"For starters you may want to change up your look. Slacks and button-down shirts may go over well in the 60s, but this is a new era."

"So, I should become black?"

Mason glared. "I would come across the table and lay hands on you, but I know you didn't mean that disrespectfully."

Tobias extended his palms in his direction. "No, no, I'm genuinely trying to find the right way to win her over. Any help you can give me, any help at all, would be greatly appreciated." He placed his hand over his heart. "Because, sir, I can't lose that woman."

Minnesota and Spacey sat inside of his car as they oversaw the Bolero drop off for a cocaine shipment at a small warehouse in Washington, D.C. When the Food Market trucks, used to conceal the coke, disappeared into the building, they exited the vehicle.

"You know you didn't have to do this with me right?" Spacey said as they walked toward the building.

"Me? You're not the only one who wants hands on in the business. Besides, I'm always the one going with pops. The only reason you a factor is because of his headaches."

"Well I'm here now." They walked into the building and Spacey removed his gun. The way he held it was as useless as a limp dick.

"I hate when you try to act hard. Maybe you should stick to counting the money. And leave the gangsta stuff to dad."

"You can never be too careful." He wielded the gun some more making it possible at any point to shoot himself in the ear.

She stopped walking. "Spacey, put the gun up. You annoying the fuck outta me."

He sighed and tucked it back into his pants, too close to his dick. They started walking again. "Anyway, I saw your friend the other day. Myrio I think. Did he get you that new car?"

"Yep...he fucks with me hard." She boasted.

"Let's just hope he keeps up the payments."

She frowned. "Excuse me?"

"It's a lease. You know that right?"

"Why would he...why would he do that?"

"Trying to impress you I guess. Did it work?"

It did at first but now she felt stupid. "It doesn't matter. As long as he doesn't expect me to make the payments, we good."

"You inviting him to your party?"

She smiled and watched as the product was removed from the truck by their workers. "Yep." She grinned. "Spacey, you should've peeped his face when he saw the invitation. That was some fly shit."

"Pops, did good with the watch invites."

"I'm telling you, it's gonna be the party of the century."

Spacey nodded. "I believe that too." He removed his phone.

"Who you texting?"

"Tobias, to let him know we're here."

They walked to the shipment to inspect the contents. "You be on his dick hard. The man wants me not you."

"He's the future." He winked. "Trust me."

CHAPTER FOUR

Nestled inside of his bed, Banks woke up in the morning with hopes for the future. Things had gone bad earlier in the week when the period should've been one of the greatest moments of his life. Instead Mason once again destroyed it all. And still that morning he woke up at least grateful that for the time being Jersey was still alive.

After slipping on his blue jeans and fresh white T, he jumped in his Benz and drove past the many soldiers that covered Jersey's property so he could see her and his infants.

He hated the setup, knowing it was just another way Mason chose to show control. He was going to scheme hard and retaliate, but he needed his new family safe first.

Irritated, Banks parked in front of the estate, took a deep breath and eased out of the car. He was experiencing one of the many headaches that plagued him lately, but he chose to ignore it. Besides, nothing was going to stop him from seeing Jersey and his sons.

When he made it to the bedroom, he was shocked to see Mason sitting in the rocker with his twin boys in his arms. While an elderly white woman with a bad yellow wig stood over top of him, as she instructed how to cradle their heads. She was Gina, the nanny.

Banks glared at Mason. "What you doing? With my kids."

Mason looked at the nanny. "You can leave us alone, Gina."

Gina smiled and walked toward the door. Stopping at Banks she said, "They're beautiful. You should be very proud."

When she left Banks said, "What you doing with my kids?"

"I don't need to tell you that's a watered-down statement."

"Watered down?"

"You and I both know these boys are not *just* yours." He kissed their foreheads. "But *ours*."

Banks' jaw twitched and he looked around. "Where is Jersey?"

"She not here."

"I get all of that. But I thought you said you weren't making any decisions right now. Are you telling me that you…that you…did you do something to my—"

"To your what?" Mason glared. "Fuck is she to you except a B.M.?"

He waved Gina inside again and she took the babies lovingly out of Mason's arms before exiting the room.

Slowly Mason rose and approached a man he knew longer than all of his sons. "Answer me this, how did you, how did you fall in love with her?"

"You don't wanna go there with me."

"Are you really gonna make me ask again? When you don't know where she is. When I can hurt her just because you disrespecting."

"She gets me. She understands me."

"I created her to be a slave." Mason said pointing at the floor. "To tend to my every need. Of course, she gets you. I taught her to obey. I mean think about it for a moment, this woman spent her entire life making sure she was accessible to me at all times. On hand and knee. Literally. That was her one and only job. Most of the times I didn't have to say what I wanted because she could read my mind."

"I know what you doing. You're trying to get me to think she's using me for revenge. That—"

"Didn't it cross your mind that you fell in love with her because she's nothing more than an avatar?" He said cutting him off. "A person who reacts based on who owns them in the minute?"

Banks felt uneasy and his headache rocked harder. "That's where you fuck up. You don't understand that she's not a slave. You treated her like shit. You talked to her like shit. And you wonder why she stopped loving you."

"I don't give a fuck about that bitch loving me!" He said pointing at the floor. "I only cared about her obeying me. And I care about your disloyalty." He paused. "Why, Banks?" His voice went lower. "Why would you...why would you do me like this? Why would you put me in a situation where I have to show you how far I would go if you pushed me?"

"Where is Jersey, Mason?" His nostrils flared.

Mason stared at him for a while. Longer than intended. But he could finally see that the Banks he knew was gone. He didn't care about their friendship anymore.

The shit hurt too.

"I have her somewhere private." He raised his chin. "Like I said, every day she will milk her breasts and that milk will be brought to our sons. Because I want them strong and healthy. And breast milk is the best way."

"How do I know you didn't kill her already?" Banks asked.

He shrugged and placed a heavy hand on his shoulder. "I guess you don't." He walked out the door.

NEXT WEEK

Mason drove down the highway thinking about his life. He couldn't believe he allowed himself to believe that despite their troubles, despite the past, his relationship with Banks was still intact.

As he blasted the radio, the last time he spoke to Banks struck him. Not only did Banks seem to not care about having children with his wife, but he appeared to not care about him at all.

Sure, they had troubles, but he didn't understand how they got so far apart. After learning that Minnesota and Arlyndo were dating, and overcoming Whoyawanmetabe at Skull Island, he thought if anything they were more solid than ever.

But Banks had proven shit was different these days.

And the energy between them felt sinister.

After pulling up in the parking lot to meet Tobias he was shocked to see him sitting in the car with his eyes closed. He figured he must've been made from a different breed. Because where Mason stomped, you could never be so comfortable in public.

Since Banks refused to drop off Mason's money any longer, he was forced to deal with Tobias. He didn't have any feelings toward him either which way, but he did consider him strange.

Easing out of his car, Mason walked to Tobias' white BMW truck and knocked on the window once. Slowly Tobias opened his eyes and unlocked the door. Mason looked around and slipped inside.

"That's how you feel?" Mason asked. "You that comfortable you can sit in your ride with your eyes closed?"

"I was meditating."

"I get all that but in your truck?" He looked around. "In a crowded mall parking lot? With my money in this bitch?"

"I do it everywhere. It's the only thing that keeps me sane."

If he wanted to risk his life that was on him. "Where my paper?"

Tobias nodded in the back.

"Aight, I'm out." Mason grabbed the duffle bag. But for some reason he didn't leave right away. "How are things with you and Minnesota?"

"Not good. She's been spending a lot of time with Myrio. I don't know but I'm pretty sure there a thing now."

"That may be true." His phone vibrated. "Hold up." Mason received a text message from Derrick and shook his head in annoyance. Lately he had been receiving so many from him that it was stifling.

"You gotta go?"

Mason stuffed his phone back into his jeans. "Nah, but listen, the only thing you need to be worried about is what you can give her better."

"That's not helping me. I'm not rich. I mean all the money I get I send back home. And it seems like Myrio is steady and stable."

"He not stable." Mason waved the air. "Just another lil' nigga we blessed up with a position that's all."

"He got her an expensive car."

"So what?" He shrugged. "He's throwing his paper around. That still don't have shit to do with you."

Tobias nodded and looked at Mason. "I don't think there's any way I could get you to cut him off financially is there?"

Mason chuckled. "I doubt that. He's one of our highest earners."

"Then there's no way I can compete. Maybe I should let her go."

"Yeah, if you can give up that easily then maybe you should. At the end of the day my niece wants a confident man. Not a nigga willing to tuck, dick and hide at the first sign of competition."

Tobias looked away. "So, what do I do?"

Mason sighed deeply and looked at his clothes. "For starters you need to change how you dress. Your gear is like a book cover. I told you last week, but you didn't listen. Now let me clean you up."

"Wait, you're going to help me buy clothes? In the—."

"Nigga, you had me meet you at a mall. I know you dry begging. Now do you want me to show you the right way or not?"

Three hours later they had been to almost every mall in the DMV area. In the end Tobias had jeans, the proper shirts and nice shoes. Although he didn't make him look too urban, Mason did find a nice middle ground that complimented his Latin steeze and his youth. After he was done Tobias felt better and more confident.

"So now what do I do?" He said after sliding on his designer spring windbreaker.

"That's the part of the game I can't give you. I will say whatever decision you make with Minnesota has to be firm. She has to know that if she wants to be with you, she has to prove it."

"I don't wanna force her."

"Your call. But every bitch I ever dated had to be shown the right way to treat me."

An hour later Tobias and Mason walked into the Louisville estate, laughing and talking about some females they met at a bar they visited. They were mother and daughter, but both looked like sisters, which was just what Mason needed.

As the two went on about the encounter, Derrick and Shay hung down the hall, watching it all.

"They seem extra close all of a sudden." She said whispering in his ear as they watched the duo head to the bar area.

"You know I texted my father six times today? He ain't hit me back once. What if something woulda happened? And now I find out he was hanging with that nigga."

"You're going to have to watch them closely."

"I know." He glared. "Cause I don't trust that mothafucka at all."

CHAPTER FIVE

Banks held his babies in his arms as they slept peacefully in the nursery, he had built for them in his mansion. Since they were three months old, he took them from Jersey's estate for the day, with plans on returning them later. The nanny Gina, who would move between his place and her estate, was very helpful and he appreciated her presence.

As he looked down at their faces he was filled with pride with a hint of rage. One of them, Ace, was light skin and possessed the same tone as Banks. The other, Walid, was tinted lightly brown and was also perfect. But in the end, both of them were mixtures of Banks and Mason combined.

"I don't know what your lives will become, but I promise to protect you with every bullet in my gun and all the power in my possession."

He had just placed his babies in their twin bassinets when Spacey walked inside the room. He stood in the doorway and smiled down at his brothers.

"When are you going to tell me where they came from?"

"You should know where babies come from by now." He winked. "But if you want, I can re-teach you the birds and the bees."

Spacey laughed. "Who was the donor and carrier?"

"When I think you can handle it, I'll tell you."

Spacey shrugged. "But they're here now. I don't think there's any better time."

Banks crossed his arms over his chest. "Everything okay? I know that look on your face. Something is serious."

"You know I have a girlfriend, right?"

Banks was aware. And although he didn't know her, he could tell they were deeply attached. "Yeah. So, what is it? You have that look in your eyes. Might as well tell me now before I drop the twins off."

"Drop them off where?"

"Spacey, what the fuck do you want?"

"Okay, okay, I'm getting married."

Banks' arms dropped at his sides as he approached him slowly. "Wait...what?"

"I'm getting married." He repeated in a blurted laugh. "Are you happy for me, pops?"

Banks was so excited he could hardly stand still. He didn't know what strange information he thought he would hit him with, but a wedding was out of the realm of possibilities.

To be honest, at first, he thought his son was gay.

Banks yanked him close and hugged him tightly. Releasing him he said, "When did you ask her? How did you know…tell me more! More than anything are you sure, son? Women can be scandalous and—"

"You know how I am, pops! I have to be sure before I make a move like this."

"Well why didn't you tell me you were going to propose? I could've helped you set things up."

"To be honest I knew the first time I met her that I was gonna make her my wife. I just got a little nudge recently."

"A little nudge?" He frowned. "From who?"

He shrugged. "Doesn't matter. But there was something about her I liked and that never changed over time. I guess my asking her to be my wife was the next logical step. I would've done it a long time ago if things were different." He looked down. "You know, with everything we got going on."

Banks realized he was speaking about their family being in the cocaine business. True, they built an empire on drugs and it wasn't anything he would want to tell a woman. And then there were all of the crimes. All of the deaths. Some may say that the Wales family was jinxed.

They may be right.

"You think ma would be happy?"

"I know she would be."

Spacey looked down and took a deep breath. "I think she would be too."

"So, when are you getting married?"

"I'm just going to do something light in September. We both agreed we don't need a lot of drama like a ceremony."

"Light?"

"Yeah we're going to the justice of the peace."

Banks frowned. "No, you're not. You're a Wales."

"I know, Pops, but—"

"We'll have the wedding here. I'll deck the house out and everything."

Spacey scratched his scalp. "But I thought you were having Minnesota's birthday party in September. She been talking about it for months."

He walked over to the bassinets and looked down at his sons. "She'll understand."

"Yeah right. Have you met your daughter ever?"

Banks looked at him. "Trust me, things will be fine. Besides, a wedding is exactly what this family needs. So, a wedding is what this family is gonna get."

Minnesota just finished making a large salad in the kitchen. Normally the chef prepared the meals, but she had been craving one so badly she wanted to make it herself. She used iceberg lettuce, onions, tomatoes, olives, shavings of carrots, eggs and even croutons. To make sure she got the taste she was aiming for, she even prepared a nice balsamic dressing to litter on top.

She was just getting ready to enjoy herself at the kitchen table when Tobias walked inside. It was strange, in the kitchen they both felt at home and as a result, they always seemed to meet up in the same place. After all she was black, and he was Latin, and for their culture's, food was life.

Before he said a word, the thing she noticed immediately was that he was dressed for his age. Off black jeans, a nice designer white T-shirt with blue Balenciaga sneakers. He didn't overdo his styles and as a result he looked just right. She even caught herself staring a bit too long.

"Where you going all dressed up and shit?" She asked, pouring the vinaigrette dressing on her salad to the point of making it too wet.

"Right now, I want to grab something to eat." He pointed at the fridge. "Mind if I join you? Maybe have a little salad?"

She shrugged as if she couldn't care less but she definitely wanted his company. "You can do whatever you want. I guess you live here or whatever."

"Doesn't have to be that way. I mean, do you want me to leave?"

"Did I say that? Anyway, everybody knows your broke ass sends all your money home. Where you gonna go?"

He laughed. "Salad?" He pointed at hers. "I always like when you make them."

"How you know it's me and not the chef?"

"Because sometimes she throws a bunch of whatever she thinks people eat into a bowl." He grabbed a plate and dished up some. "And its usually too much food and you can't catch all of the flavors. But yours is always just right."

"If you say so."

He sat across from her. "So, what you got going on today?"

"I'm not going out with you, Tobias."

Her comment was meant to hurt him, but he didn't seem phased. Actually, he didn't seem bothered at all. And for a moment she wondered if it was true that clothing made the man.

"That's good." He winked. "Wherever you're going, I hope you have a nice time."

She frowned. "A friend."

"Huh?"

"I'm going out with a friend."

He nodded and ate more salad. "Have fun."

The fact that he didn't question her more bothered her a little and she wasn't sure why.

She was about to warm up some homemade soup when Banks walked into the kitchen. "Glad you're both here. We're having dinner tomorrow. Make sure you're both home. I have an important announcement to make."

Banks' mood seemed happy and upbeat so neither was worried. "Sounds good, sir. What time should I return? I have plans later."

Minnesota wondered what *plans* he had, and jealousy consumed her, but she decided to remain silent.

"Seven o'clock works fine."

"Do you mind if I bring a friend?" Minnesota asked, hoping to get Tobias a little roused. She looked at him, but he didn't gaze her way.

"Somebody on my approved list?" Banks asked.

"Kinda."

Before answering Banks looked at Tobias. He wondered if she was trying to mess with his mind or simply get him jealous. If she was doing either, truthfully, he wanted no parts. After all, he liked the young man and still held hopes for their union when his daughter was of age.

But when Tobias gave a nod that he was okay, Banks looked at Minnesota. "I'll need more details on him, but for now I'll say yes." He turned to walk away but turned back around. "And somebody tell Shay. She's still a part of this family too."

All night Banks thought about Jersey. Although he knew they could never be a couple, it bothered him that her fate, wherever she was, was his fault. So, he decided to pop up over her house again.

Mason still had it heavily armed.

When he pulled up to Jersey's estate, he was secretly hoping he would find her there. *Maybe Mason allowed her to return at night, from whatever hole he had her posted.* He thought. And at the same time, he realized it was an impossibility. Mason made his stance clear. He would never allow them to be together.

Walking into the house, when he made it to the nursery once again Mason was rocking in the chair, holding their sons. It was clear in that moment that he was intent on bonding with them.

"Look at my seeds." Mason bragged. "Aren't they perfect?"

He acted as if he'd given birth. "Where is she?"

"The milk is here if that's what you're asking."

"You know it's not. I wanna know where Jersey is."

"I can't believe after all this time you still ask me about her. Haven't you learned by now, I will tell you what I want you to know when I want you to know it?"

"Keeping us apart won't matter, Mason. I'ma still have feelings for her regardless."

"Unresolved feelings."

"Whatever you wanna call them." Banks shrugged. "I just want you to know that this...whatever it is, ain't working. I will find a way to get her back. You know that about me."

"You won't be successful."

Banks glared. "It's like...it's like you want me to hate you or something. Is that your goal? Because it's working."

"Brother, the last thing I want you to do is hate me. But I realize it's where you feel most natural don't you? Things going smooth with us never worked for you. You prefer fury. You prefer to hate me because it's too hard to love me. You think by doing all of this...by disrespecting me and fucking my wife, that I will finally turn my back on you like everyone else in your life. Guess what, I will never turn my back on you."

"Whatever, Mason."

"One of these days you're going to regret how you're treating me, Banks. Think about it for a minute. I'm the most hated man alive. What will you do if something happened to me on these streets? What will you do if I'm not there to let you know that no matter what you're not alone?"

"Right now, I wouldn't care what happened to you. And that's being real."

Mason shuffled a little. "You, you really mean that?"

Silence.

Mason took a deep breath and looked down at their children. He placed them in their bassinets and walked toward Banks. "Why did you name them Walid and Ace?"

Banks folded his arms over his chest. Mason was never supposed to know about the names because he was never supposed to know about the babies. And yet he realized by the question that he already had the answer.

"What difference does it make why I named them?"

"You gave them the same names we used to call ourselves as kids. When we didn't want nobody knowing who we really were. Did you think I would forget?"

It was true.

Whenever they used to get in trouble in the streets and people asked them their names, Banks would call himself Ace and Mason would call himself Walid. And although time passed, Banks always like the names. And had Mason not been in the picture when he had his son's with Bethany, Spacey would've been called Walid and Joey would've been Ace.

Mason smiled when he caught the expression on his face. "You see what I'm saying? I am you and you are me. The sooner you realize that the sooner we can put this shit behind us."

"We will never be what you want, nigga. Ever."

Mason smiled brightly. "I heard you're having a dinner party tonight."

"You not invited."

Mason chuckled and walked to the door. "I'ma let you spend some alone time with our son's. It's best that both of us get to know them anyway. Since we family and all."

CHAPTER SIX

A warm day in Towson Maryland, it was raining after Myrio and Minnesota left the movie theater. Making sure she remained dry, using an umbrella, he walked her to the car, tossed it in the back and pulled off.

Sitting in the passenger seat she looked at him repeatedly. Myrio was fine. But more than it all he was confident, and that did something for her rebel heart.

"Why you over there looking at me like that?" He asked slyly.

"So, what, I can't look at you now?"

"I'm not saying all that, but you staring me down like you about to eat me up or something." He chuckled.

"I'm trying to figure you out that's all." She crossed her legs. "Because I feel like there's something else with you."

"I wish you stop doing that. Not everything needs to be analyzed."

"Not everything needs to be analyzed." She repeated. "You sound crazy."

"I'm serious. Are you a grown woman or not? Because grown women don't feel the need to break down every moment, because things are what they are."

"Come on now, don't play me."

"Answer me! Are you a woman or not?"

"Oh, I forgot. I haven't let you fuck, so you think I'm a dude. That's why you talking wild."

"You mean I haven't let *you* fuck yet."

She busted out in laughter and quieted down. "You know I'm a woman, Myrio. I just, I just wanna know more about you that's all."

"Okay, I'm feeling you right now. In a way I haven't felt in a long time. Shouldn't that be enough?"

"Okay so let's do this."

"I'm listening." He merged onto the highway.

"What are you looking for? And don't give me that game about you're going with the flow, Myrio. I really want to know."

"Are you going to be able to take it if I tell you?"

"I'm here ain't I?"

"I'm looking for a powerful bitch. Somebody who knows what she wants and is not afraid to get it. At the same time, I want her to be submissive to me. And only me. Some women can't deal with that, but I'd like to let them know upfront what I want anyway."

"Is that why I had to beat you down to get an answer? Because you upfront?"

He laughed. "I like what I like. But I had to be cautious telling you because, you're the kind of girl who'll probably tell everything."

She frowned. "What does that mean?"

"Your father is my boss. That's important. But I need to know what happens between us stays between us."

She sighed. "I'm getting tired of people bringing up my father. What about keeping the focus on me? What about what I want?"

He looked at her and could tell he hit a sore spot. "Listen, I don't know how it would be to be raised with money. I'm a first-generation rich nigga. So, I apologize if I'm coming at you the wrong way. At the same time dealing with you could be bad for my pockets. All I'm asking for is the freedom to tell you what I need and want without it leaving the two of us."

"My father didn't seem to stop you before."

"He's not stopping me now, unless you let him." He paused. "I mean, can you handle the truth? Can I trust you?"

"Myrio, handling the truth is not an issue. I need the truth. But I also need to be around somebody who is there for me. And only me. So, the question is, can I trust *you*?"

Dinner was served and everybody was present. In attendance was Spacey, his fiancé Lila, Joey, who hadn't been around in a while, Tobias, Minnesota and Myrio.

Everyone was in all black.

After the first course was done, Banks decided to bring up the purpose of the meal.

He rose. "Settle down everyone."

The room grew silent.

"We've had a rough few years. Lost a lot of people and I'm sure we'll lose many more along the way."

Everyone was shooketh.

Why lose more?

"But what has kept me grounded…what has kept me focused is this family. I'm nothing without family. And that includes my daughters and sons."

"Dad, you're scaring me now." Minnesota said.

"No need to be scared. This all good news." He clapped once. "Spacey getting married."

Minnesota and Joey were shocked, although relieved he wasn't giving them bad news. This they could handle. The room grew excited with cheers and gasps. After giving Spacey and Lila hugs everyone settled down and returned to their seats.

"I have more." Banks continued. "They're getting married here. In September."

Minnesota glared. "Here? What...what about my party?"

"We'll celebrate a few days after the wedding."

"A few days after. But invitations went out already. You even paid for the watches. I told the few friends I have." She placed her hand over her heart. "Dad, I've been planning this party for months, don't do this."

"You just said you haven't invited many friends."

"Still, you promised me a celebration. You promised to make my day worth it and instead you plan a wedding?"

"I can have my wedding another day, dad." Spacey said. "It's not a big deal."

"No, you can't! We're doing it in September! Period."

Minnesota was embarrassed as she sat back in her seat. "When are my feelings going to be acknowledged in this family?"

"Oh, here we go," Joey shook his head.

"What?"

Joey laughed. "Your feelings. How you sound? For the first thirteen years you were born your opinion was the only one that mattered in this house."

"I'm not that selfish person anymore."

"Well prove it and stop tripping!" Joey continued. "Because I think it's a good idea for us to have a wedding too. I'm sick of all the drama and deaths in this family." He looked down as thoughts of his mother entered his mind. "You could...you could have a party any day."

"You good, man?" Spacey asked touching his brother's hand.

"I'm good." Joey pulled back.

"I can't believe I keep letting my family build my hopes up for nothing." Minnesota continued. "I'm starting to realize that since ma died, no one cares about me in this house anymore."

"Minnesota, I know you're sad, but this is important for us all." Banks said. "A party is something we can do at any time. You have a birthday each year."

"You mean like Harris? And mama?"

He glared. "You know what I mean!"

"No, I don't! Promises were made that aren't being kept. And I'm tired of it."

Before he could answer the maid entered the dining room. "Sir, Mason is at the door to see you."

"Fuck does he want?" He said mostly to himself.

Annoyed, he quickly rose and rushed to the foyer.

Standing by the door was Mason and Jersey. They were fit for the evening in the color code. Mason in a tux, he had her in a black dress that ate most of her curves in a seductive way. Even her make-up was done so professionally, it almost shielded the fact that she was scared.

Banks approached her. "Are you...are you okay?" He touched her forearm lightly.

"Hold up, man," Mason said with a palm to Banks' chest. "It's rude to touch another man's date. Don't you know that by now?"

Banks glared and took two steps back. Whatever kind of game he was playing, Banks wanted no part of it. "What's this about, man?"

"Like I said earlier, I heard you were having a dinner party. So, I brought a date."

His emotions swirled.

On one hand he wanted desperately to see her but on the other hand he hated Mason for this move. I mean, were they fucking?

Focusing on his love he said, "Are you hurt, Jersey?"

She looked back at Mason and then Banks. "No, but I, but I miss you so much."

Neither could see how Mason felt inside but he definitely saw black upon hearing such powerful words pour from her heart to Banks. They really could care less that he was there.

"Are you going to invite us in or not?" Mason asked through clenched teeth.

Five minutes later after hanging in the foyer, Banks, Jersey and Mason walked into the dining room. Like Banks, the others were surprised to see them.

"Are you gonna tell them about you and my wife?" Mason asked Banks before even taking a seat.

"Mason, please don't." Jersey said.

"Please don't?" Mason laughed sitting down. He didn't even bother to pull out Jersey's seat. She had to find her own way. "But you already did. Both of you." He looked at Banks. "Are you gonna tell them about you and my wife? Or should I?"

"Dad, what's going on?" Spacey asked.

"Yeah, pops, I'm confused." Joey added.

Banks felt ill but needed to be real. "Jersey and I…we…I mean…"

"Your father fucking my wife." Mason laughed as he reached for a roll.

"What?" Spacey said. "Why? I don't get it."

"It's too much to tell you right now."

"So, you were doing this when ma was alive?" Joey asked with a lowered brow.

"Yes."

"Wow," Joey said shaking his head. "I can't believe this shit."

Minnesota covered her mouth while Myrio rubbed her back.

On the other side of the table Tobias was sick with jealousy. But what could he do? It appeared that she had chosen what she wanted. At that time, he reasoned that if they were meant to be, they would.

Mason smiled after disrupting the house. "So, now that that's out the way, are we going to eat or what?"

Banks nodded and grabbed the fork. But everybody around him knew Banks was knocked out of his comfort zone. Which was a place he preferred not to be.

"Aren't you going to tell your friends about Spacey too?" Minnesota asked with an attitude. "And you're broken promise to me."

"This dinner party is about my son. He's, he's getting married."

"Wow, good news," Mason said as he went to shake Spacey's hand. "That's what we need around here."

Spacey shook his hand and smiled.

"So, when is the wedding day?" Mason continued to eat.

"Soon." Banks said providing zero deets.

He didn't want anyone knowing outside of his immediate family about the wedding. Especially Mason Louisville.

And so, they ate in silence wondering what would happen next.

After dinner, Tobias was walking to his bedroom when Spacey bounced up to him. "That was crazy wasn't it?" Spacey asked.

Tobias stopped. "What you mean? With Jersey and Banks?"

"No, with Minnesota and Myrio."

Tobias shuffled a little, suddenly feeling uncomfortable. "There's nothing I can do. She wants what she wants."

"Are you sure?"

"What do you mean?"

"I can kill him."

Tobias' eyes widened. He didn't know Spacey to be a gangster and his eyes told him he still wasn't.

"Listen, don't do anything like that for me. Shit will work out as it should. It always does. Trust me."

CHAPTER SEVEN

Mason and Jersey drove quietly down the highway after leaving the dinner party. Originally, when he went to Banks' house, she was so excited she felt sick to the stomach just thinking about seeing his face. He had to pull over so she could vomit on the side of the road or she would destroy her designer gown. She was a big ball of mess, especially considering the fact that originally, he didn't tell her where he was going.

Instead, Mason walked into the room she was staying, tossed her a new dress and told her to make it work. An hour later a makeup artist came and beat her face to perfection. But seeing Banks, and the way he looked at her, only reinforced how she felt.

She was in love.

Banks was too.

"What are you going to do with me?" Jersey asked quietly, as her hands laid heavily in her lap. "And the twins."

"You don't get the right to ask questions." He continued to maneuver the car down the road. "I should be killing you right now."

"Mason, you can't do this. You have to understand how wrong this is on many levels. I know you don't like what has become of us but keeping me away from Derrick, and the twins is terrible."

He shifted a little. "Now you worried about your kids? Fuck you, slut."

"Mason—"

"What did you do to him?"

"What?"

"You heard me. What did you do to Banks to make him this way?"

She frowned. "I didn't do anything to him. We got together at a time when we both needed each other. Neither of us wanted it to be the way that it was but things happen. And I'm sorry. He chose me."

"For now." Mason said. "And how long has it been going on?" He yanked the wheel to the right to bypass a car. The quick motion was mostly done out of anger.

"Banks and I didn't...we didn't fall in love until after we left Wales Island."

"I don't believe you. The way ya'll niggas acting, it had to be longer than that."

"I understand why you feel that way, but it really is the truth."

He looked over at her, secretly wanting to beat the beauty away he felt caused his friend to lose reason. He even thought about putting a gun to her eardrums and pulling the trigger. To be honest, technically he hadn't said what he really planned to do with her so would anyone be surprised if Jersey Louisville popped up dead?

"You going to tell me what's on your mind or you going to be quiet all night?" Myrio asked as they sat on the patio overlooking the Wales estate. "Because I ain't come out here for the silent treatment."

"Why didn't you defend me in the house? To my father."

He frowned. "Wait, you wanted me to speak on a situation I didn't have the full details on? To my boss at that?"

She didn't but she did want him to be on her side at the very least. "You see how they disrespect me?"

He stuffed his hands into his pockets. "I wouldn't call it disrespect."

She looked at him and her mouth fell open. "If that wasn't disrespect, what is?"

He sat next to her. "You're young. And the young are often overlooked."

"Okay, you gotta explain better because I'm really irritated now."

"There's this misconception that 'cause you haven't lived long you aren't smart. In some cases, it's true. So, it wasn't disrespect. They just don't take you seriously."

"So now my family doesn't love me?"

"I've made myself clear, Minnesota. Don't turn around my words. And I'm not the enemy. I think you're used to people leading you on and telling you what you wanna hear. But that will never be the case with me. It's important that you know that upfront."

She looked down. "Sometimes a girl likes to know you're on her side, Myrio."

"Are you a girl or woman? Because if I recall, we had a whole conversation on the way over here about that shit."

"Sometimes you get on my nerves." She smiled.

"I think we have chemistry." He shrugged.

"So, I say you get on my nerves and you think we have chemistry?" She shook her head softly. "For a man who defines himself as saying what's on his mind you sure do beat around the bush."

"They say we dislike what's closest to ourselves. So, if I'm getting on your nerves that's the first clue we mesh."

"For me it's to be determined."

"I guess we'll see."

Minnesota walked to her room after escorting Myrio off the property.

After the day she had, she was exhausted, hurt and angry. And despite beefing with Myrio, he somehow made things right by being in her presence. And still, there was an area in her heart that was reserved for Tobias. As the stars twinkled, she was hoping he'd be more jealous. More receptive. Instead as she sat at dinner with another man, he didn't even look her way.

When she made it to her room, she paused when she saw Joey inside and next to her dresser. He was shutting it and acting suspiciously. Confused, she walked deeper inside the room and slammed the door loudly.

"Fuck are you doing in here?"

He turned around quickly and placed his arms behind his back. "I was looking to see if you had any condoms."

She didn't believe him. It was all in his eyes. "You've never gotten condoms from me before. Why start now?"

He rolled his eyes. "Stop making such a big deal outta shit. I came in here to see if you had some and you didn't, so it's done."

Her gaze stayed on him a bit longer. After observing him for what seemed like forever, what she saw on her brother's face caused her heart to ache. She squinted. "Hold up, are you on drugs?"

"How the fuck you sound?" Suddenly he couldn't stand still. "Of course, I'm not on drugs!"

"I don't believe you."

"You don't have to. I'm telling you I'm not and that should be the end of it!"

As he moved to leave, she grabbed his wrist, while looking deeper into his eyes. Although she had been around drug dealers all of her life and not necessarily drug users, she felt in her heart she was right. At one point she had a few friends who rolled in the pill popping crowd, but Joey looked down and out. It was obvious that he was not only a user but an addict.

"Joey, you can't be serious." She trembled. "This is really gonna be your story?"

"Don't go telling rumors on me, Minnie. I'm warning you." He stormed out.

Walking to her drawer, she pushed around her undies and her diary and moved to the envelope she kept in the back. It was gone and so was her money.

Banks was getting ready for bed when Minnesota knocked softly on his door. Seeing her face on the monitor of the camera he had installed, he sat on the edge of the bed.

He didn't have time for any of her shit. "Come inside."

She walked in and closed the door.

"I don't wanna argue today." He said. "I gotta see the twins tomorrow."

"I don't want to argue either." She crossed her arms over her chest.

He looked at her closer. "Listen, I know I told you we would have that party. And I had all intentions on doing it. But things happened and—."

"If you know you told me why would you do this? At the last minute. It's so embarrassing. I gave Myrio the watch and everything."

"Let him keep it."

"Daddy!"

"I thought you didn't want to argue."

"I don't but...I mean..."

"Like I said already, we really need this for us. And I know you think coming in here will get me to change my mind. But I assure you it won't. Besides, I've given you a lot of attention around here. Time to spread the love."

She wasn't interested in going any further. It was time to cut him deep. "I think Joey is using drugs."

He frowned. "What you talking about using drugs?"

"I walked in on him going through my drawers. When I went to investigate after he left, I realized my money was gone."

He stood up and paced a little. Pausing he said, "Joey doesn't have to steal from you. Or anybody else for that matter. I just gave him money yesterday."

She shrugged. "Well how often you give him cash?"

He thought about it a few seconds. "Lately it's been every day. So, again, there's no need to steal."

A deep breath. "Well, I think you need to pay closer attention to your children, dad. Since you so busy! I know what I saw. The rest is up to you." She walked out.

Bolero had just finished ensuring that Banks and Mason received their next shipment and now he wanted to share a meal with his best workers. The old friends were seated in front of him in a restaurant that he ordered shut down for the meeting while Tobias sat on his left, preparing to feast.

"Leave us alone," Bolero told Tobias.

"I thought we were about to eat." He frowned.

Bolero stared at him and Tobias got up and left with his head hung low.

Banks wasn't feeling how he treated him one bit. "He seems disappointed."

"He likes it a lot with you, Banks." Bolero cut into his meat. "Good job."

Banks nodded. "He's a good kid."

"True. And although I don't have the best relationship with him, it's important that he's at ease."

"So, you are admitting he's your son now and not your nephew?" Banks asked sarcastically.

Bolero smiled but chose to ignore the question. With a deep breath he said, "I don't have to tell you that I'm very happy with production lately. The repeated orders prove that you two know what you're doing."

"When it comes to coke, we the best." Mason said. "Still nice to hear though."

Bolero laughed. "I didn't know you were one for compliments. I would've given you some sooner."

Mason grinned. "I like hearing anything pertaining to production and money. I always say give me my flowers while I'm alive."

He nodded. "Okay, I'll remember that in the future. But like I said, you both are doing very well."

Although Mason was conversational, it didn't take Bolero long to see that Banks appeared to be somewhere else mentally. "Is something on your mind, Banks?"

"He's fine." Mason said.

"Then he can answer for himself."

Banks sat back in his seat not in the mood for conversation. "I'm good. But if I'm being honest, I have twin sons I wanna get back to. Are we done here?"

"Oh, I heard about that." Bolero said.

Banks glared. "How did you hear about that?"

Bolero looked at Mason and Banks reached yet another level of anger having gotten his answer.

"When are you going to realize you talk too much, nigga?" Banks asked Mason.

"It ain't about talking too much. The man asked what was going on in my life when we had a quick call the other day and I told him about my kids. I'm proud. You should be too."

In that moment, Banks knew Mason's motives. He was deliberately trying to send him over the edge. But he also knew he had to keep his composure in front of the Plug. Because Banks was definitely plotting revenge, but as always, it had to be at the right time.

"Is this meeting over or what?" Banks asked.

"Why you being rude?" Mason smiled. "The man was simply mentioning our boys. Aren't you going to respond?"

Banks jaw twitched. "Is the meeting over, Bolero?"

Now Bolero could see why their time together had been so intense. The old friends were at odds. Which to Bolero was bad for business. Especially considering all the good money involved.

"I don't know what's going on. And I don't care. Let me just say whatever is happening it better not interfere with operations."

"I don't know about this nigga, but have I ever let you down?" Banks asked.

Bolero sighed. He hadn't. "Yes, the meeting is over. For now."

After they left the restaurant and Banks headed to his car, Mason walked closely behind like a shadow. "What's on your mind?"

Banks turned around and faced him. "*What's on my mind?* Nigga, we not friends no more. So, whatever's going on with me ain't none of your concern."

"You that torn up over a bitch?"

"Listen, we just business partners. You got it? We not going back to that other shit we did when we were kids. Ever!"

"There you go again saying shit you don't mean."

"Let me put it like this, I regret the day you left that building I blew up. Because if you were inside, you'd be dead instead of ruining my life. So, stay the fuck up out my face."

Mason felt gut punched. "You that mad you would wish death on me?"

"I done told you that already. We done, done. I'm just waiting for the day that somebody can take your ass out."

"I'ma let that go."

Banks walked closer. "You don't have to let it go. But let it sink in. If somebody else don't kill you, I might have to do it myself." Banks climbed in his car and pulled off.

Mason and Tobias sat in his lounge playing chess. Since they developed this organic friendship, they spent a lot of time on the game. Mason considered himself smart, but Tobias appeared to have a natural knack at the art, and it frustrated him slightly.

"You gonna make a move?" Tobias asked looking at the board.

Mason looked up at him and glared. "Do I bother you when you're thinking?"

He smiled. "No. But the thing is, I don't think you're thinking. I think you're stalling and there's a difference."

Mason chuckled because he was right. But he wasn't going to let him know. At the end of the day he was starting to come to terms with Banks and his bond being officially over and shit was hard.

Still in his head, he moved in a position where he exposed his Queen. And just like that Tobias yelled, "Checkmate."

Defeated, Mason flopped back in his chair and rubbed his hands down his face.

"Now I will admit that I'm better at this than you, but something seems way off tonight." Tobias said.

"It's nothing I wanna talk about."

He leaned closer. "You sure?"

"Yeah. Let's skip the subject. What's up with you and Minnesota?" He got up and poured two glasses of whiskey.

"I'm done. I think she really likes Myrio."

He frowned and handed him a glass before taking a seat. "Wait, Banks likes him too? Sounds odd. He don't fuck with nobody."

"Banks is doing a lot of things he doesn't normally do these days. Complains of headaches a lot too. It's like, I know it's him, but he still seems off. The only time he slows down is when he's around the twins."

"Yeah, they're perfect." He said proudly.

Tobias put his glass down. "I don't talk a lot about this, I guess because nobody officially told me. I just heard things through being around. Even Minnesota, Joey and Spacey seem to be out of the loop. But, um—."

"You wanna get to your point, nigga?"

Tobias laughed. "Was Banks really your girlfriend when you were kids?"

"Wow, I didn't think you would hit me with that."

"If I'm out of line don't worry about answering."

He sighed. "What I tell you about not standing your ground?"

"Okay, was he really your girlfriend back in the day? Because when I see him, I can't imagine any moment where he would be female."

"You're not alone." Mason sighed deeply. "The world sees him now as male. But I still see the past." He sighed. "But yeah, it's true. Was the first girl I loved. And if I'm being honest, the only one."

"Do you *really* love him, or do you think you love him?"

"First of all, I don't love him in that way anymore."

Tobias didn't believe him. "Okay."

"But I'm going to always care about him."

"So why are you moving like this then?"

Mason frowned. "What that mean?"

"You know how he feels about Jersey. And you're still willing to anger him by keeping them apart."

"What happened to you understanding my point of view? The man straight fucking my wife. Based on how she's acting, he's fucking her well."

Tobias smiled. "This is different."

"Fuck that mean?"

"It's just that I didn't think you prided yourself on being a victim."

"Don't get killed."

Tobias laughed. "I just think with Joey possibly being on drugs and the headaches Banks has been having lately, he needs Jersey. You are making matters—."

He sat up. "What you just say about Joey?"

Tobias moved uneasily having said too much. "Well, I don't know the details, but Minnesota caught him in her room. Going through her drawers looking for money. But even before that I heard talk about him on the streets. He's using opioids. But that was before he found heroin."

Mason's fists clutched. "You know the young bull out there wrong and you didn't do anything about it?"

Tobias glared. "After I got facts I went to work. Every person he bought from I threatened within every inch of their lives. But I didn't want to bring Banks more trouble. I dealt with him myself. So now where you could get a pill for $25, he has to pay upwards of two hundred by sneaking around."

"Who he copping from now?"

He shrugged. "I don't know. But I have definitely been looking and asking around. If I find out they're gone too."

Mason got up and stormed toward the door.

"What are you about to do?"

Joey was in his favorite bar, a hole in the wall in Reisterstown Maryland. He had been drinking and even popped a few pills when he decided it was time to go to the apartment, he now stayed in with this hood rat name Rebecca.

The moment he walked out the door he was yanked inside of a white Mercedes truck by two large men. In that moment, he saw his life flash before his eyes until he focused on Mason's angry face.

Mason's soldiers stayed outside of the truck, on guard.

Seeing a familiar face, Joey looked around slightly relieved. "What...what's this about, Unc?"

Mason glared. "So, you getting high now?"

"Who told you that? Minnesota?" He frowned. "Because it ain't like that."

"Then what is it like?"

"It's about me going through a lot of shit. It's about my mind being messed up. I lost my brother. And my mother's death is on my head! Everybody feels that way. And I can't handle this the way everybody else does. And I know you don't understand what it feels like to be in this pain. But—."

"You have no idea what I been going through." Mason roared. "You don't think I tried to kill myself? You don't think I made decisions not to live anymore? Every day it's work just to get up, but I do, nigga. Every day."

Joey looked down. "So, what, so what changed your mind?"

"My sons. And now the twins."

Joey frowned. "The twins! Why them?"

It was at that time that Mason realized he didn't know about him fathering his brothers. It was also evident that Banks picked and chose who he told the secret. He must've been ashamed after all.

And then something happened.

Something Mason couldn't put into words.

He snapped.

At that moment, he didn't see Joey anymore. He saw himself when he was younger. He saw all of the things he'd done currently and in the past. And so, he stole Joey in the face.

Upon impact, the back of his head knocked against the window, shattering the glass like a spider web. Instead of stopping, he hit him again. Over and over and over until Joey's face was so beaten, he could hardly see out of his eyes.

When he was done, he shook his throbbing hand. "If I catch you copping from anybody, next time I'm gonna kill you and dump you in a lot. Now get the fuck outta my truck, dopehead."

CHAPTER EIGHT

Banks was on the way to Jersey's estate. He was tired of being controlled and at the same time realized for the moment there was nothing else he could do. Nothing would keep him from his sons.

When he walked past the many guards that Mason hired, and into the house, he was surprised to see Jersey sitting in the rocker nursing the babies from her actual breasts instead of bottles.

Confused he walked inside and closed the door.

Rushing up to her, he dropped to his knee and touched her leg. "What's going on?" He looked behind him. "Are you, are you okay?"

"I'm fine." She smiled, tears rolling down her cheeks. "Really."

"So, why are you here?" His heart banged heavily in his chest.

"I don't know." She shrugged. "He just let me go." She smiled happily.

"Let you go." He whispered. "Without a reason?"

"I'm as shocked as you are, Banks. He had me in this apartment complex in DC. It wasn't bad but it, but it wasn't home." Her words exited in a mixture of cries, laughter and relief. "And this morning he, he, he came in and said I was free to leave. I asked him what about the babies and he said I could keep them with me. Although…" She looked down.

"What is it?" He frowned.

"He said he had all intentions on remaining in the boy's lives."

He rose. "Does he expect you to go back to him? Because that'll never happen. I'll kill him before I—."

"No, Banks." She shook her head quickly from left to right. "He let me go. Really."

"Why though? This nigga not chivalrous. He ain't the type of dude who relents."

"This time I think he's really done. We can be together. Finally."

He paced a few feet. "I, I don't get it. The last time I saw him I wished ill will. And I don't take it back."

"Well maybe he feels bad."

"Jersey, there is no way he feels bad." He rushed toward the door.

"Where are you going?"

"Just stay right here."

Banks exited the room and walked quickly past the guards. A few of them, which he knew, he asked if Mason was around. Each said the same thing.

No.

Still, he searched every end of that property and didn't spot Mason Louisville or a threat. He even considered a bomb possibly going off, destroying himself, Jersey and the babies.

But again, there was nothing to be found.

In the end Banks reasoned that whatever Mason had planned it would be coming later. So, reentering the room, he walked up to her and helped her to her feet. Holding one of the babies carefully he said, "Let's go."

"Did you find anything?" She asked.

"No. But I don't trust this place anymore."

As they moved toward the door she said, "I really think we free. I feel it in my heart."

"If it's true, let's get out of here before he changes his mind."

Security covered the Wales estate as Banks and Jersey lie in bed. Even though they were together Banks was still uneasy. His heart and mind felt a plan was coming on and that he didn't have the details. He knew his ex-friend enough to know that this was bad.

A soft knock rapped on the door.

"Come in," Banks said. He was lying face up, with a hand behind his head as he stared at the ceiling.

The door opened.

It was Gina, the nanny. Since Banks built a bond with her over the months, he decided she should live with them. Besides, she'd been there a lot. "I'm preparing the babies for bed. Did you want me to wait before I put them to sleep?"

Jersey smiled. "No but thank you anyway."

She nodded and walked out, leaving Banks back to his wild thoughts.

What was Mason up to?

Jersey snuggled closely at his side. "You don't know how much I missed you."

Her voice brought him back to the present. He raised her chin and kissed her lips. "I can't believe you're here. If I wasn't thinking about you, I was thinking about our sons. So, this is insane. I actually convinced myself that I would have to kill him to get you back."

"I wish you stop saying that."

His voice rose. "What you mean stop saying that? He was fucking with you. Fucking with us."

She shook her head. "You'll never be able to kill him. You care too much."

"If you think that, then you don't know me as good as you think you do."

"I know you both enough to realize that the world may blow up, but you two will always find a reason to reconnect."

He positioned his body to look into her eyes. "Maybe in the past, but that was before Mason violated. Look at what he did. He couldn't stand that you and I were willing to be happy over everything else. So much that he actually mixed in our baby situation."

"But they're beautiful." She smiled. "Couldn't be more perfect. Maybe it was a blessing."

"That's not the fucking point!" He stood up. "It's just another way of him controlling me." His head throbbed and he rubbed his temples. "Of being involved. I wanted babies with you alone."

"Banks, what's going on with the headaches?"

"I'm fine." He thought about Mason again. "But I won't let him hurt you."

She wished he would stop with his obsession.

"I thought the same thing. But if he wanted to do something, he would have done it already. But he didn't. Be glad, Banks."

Banks nodded but looked past her at the wall. "I get it now. He'll probably be over here every day trying to get on my nerves and shit. Talking about he wanna see the boys when he just wanna see me. But I'm not gonna let that upset me. I'm gonna keep the peace until I come up with another plan to get us out of here." He rubbed his throbbing temples. "Maybe get another island somewhere."

She sighed. "Banks, I don't wanna run. I wanna be here for Derrick, the twins and Howard when he returns."

Banks shifted, because he alone knew he killed Howard months ago. "Did you fuck Mason or something? Is that what's going on? Is that why you're protecting him?"

"What, no!"

"So, what did he do to convince you he done with me? With us? I mean, come on, Jersey. Think. That nigga is sick."

She sat up in bed. "I am considering everything. I just, I just think I know the different versions of him. This felt unlike any I've seen in the past."

"I wish I could have your naive way of thinking."

She stared at him for a few moments. "What does that mean?"

"You have a whimsical view of life. You don't get niggas out here. But I do. And men like Mason don't change overnight. They're not capable. He's definitely up to something. My only issue is what."

"Banks!"

"It's true. Seems like every time I let my guards down, every time I...I...I...I mean..." Banks' mood grew dark and suddenly he resembled a wild man. Wide eyes and a thin sheen of sweat dressed his forehead.

"Banks, you're scaring me."

He rushed to the bed and sat next to her. "Don't be afraid. I would never hurt you."

"By driving yourself crazy you are. I mean, do you really wanna move through life trying to plan for everything? Trying to see everybody's next move?"

"Yes. I do. I have to."

"Okay, what if he is up to something? Don't you want to spend our last moments together making it count?" She placed her hand over her heart. "I have four sons left. And what I want to do now is spend time with them. We need to love them. And protect them."

"Even Derrick? After everything he did to you?"

"Especially Derrick. Because he was reaching out in his own way and I wasn't there." She touched his hand. "I had a dream about him the other day. And in this dream, he was being followed by a dark presence. And I knew it was a dream but as I was sitting there, I couldn't help but feel like it was real. God brought me home."

"Don't bring God into this."

"I'm serious. There are certain people in your life who God gifts you. Now I'm not saying I'm a good mother. I'm not saying I have all the answers either. But I feel like I haven't said what needs to be said to my son to let him know that despite everything, I'm still here."

He stood up again. "Some things I can't forgive. Ever."

She rose and walked him back to the bed. They sat on the edge, looking at one another. But it was obvious that even though they were face to face, he was looking through her again, still thinking about Mason.

"Can we spend whatever time we have together just being in love? Just holding each other. Just, just remembering the time we had before Mason found out. I think that's how we get back to us. That's how we get back to the good things. Not by obsessing over Mason's every move. Because at the end of the day, you'll never know what he's thinking. Even if he tells you."

Silence.

"Banks," she touched the side of his face, "are you listening?"

He nodded. "Yeah."

"Can we get back to us?"

"Nah. Not until I find out what's up."

She was sick of him. "I'm going to see my son tomorrow."

He glared. “Don’t go to that house.” He stood up and walked out of the room.

CHAPTER NINE

It was a bit cool outside as Mason cruised down the street with Dasher in his passenger seat. They went to a bar earlier that evening and now was on the way to get some dinner. She was a cute little thing, about twenty-six years old to be exact. And although she was younger there was something about her that was very familiar.

He just couldn't put his finger on what.

"Why you keep looking at me like that?" She smiled, after closing her compact mirror and dropping it in her purse.

"So, I can't look at you now?" He asked, as his eyes alternated from the dark road to her pretty face.

"I won't say all that." She crossed her legs. "It's just that the stare is intense. Like you're trying to read every thought I've ever had."

He nodded. "I like what I see."

She stared at him a bit long. "I think you're mysterious. And I like that about you. Most of the men I've dated are so high strung. Agitated. And on edge. But you're the most laid-back person I know. It's calming."

He laughed.

"What's funny?"

"If you knew me, you wouldn't say that. Matter of fact, I don't know anybody who would call me easy going."

"So, you're putting on a façade for me?"

"Nah, I wouldn't necessarily say a facade. I'm too old for that anyway. It's just that me being laid back is not something I'm known for. But I'm trying to change." He nodded. "Trying to change a lot of shit actually."

"Why?"

"I think you get to a point where you just get tired. Tired of fighting. Tired of worrying about things that don't matter. Don't get it twisted, I'll still do what need be done. And I'ma leave that comment at that. But at the end of it all I'm looking for smoother days."

"Have you lost a lot?"

"Enough. More than I care to admit. A lot of people I fucked with either died or betrayed me." He thought about Banks and his wife, who technically he was still married to.

"I'll never betray you."

He smiled. "Don't make promises you can't keep."

"Never."

Thirty minutes later, Dasher and Mason joined Tobias and his new female friend, Alexis at inexpensive restaurant in Georgetown in Washington D.C.

She was a cutie, Black and Hispanic and owned several hair salons in and around the city.

The conversation between the four was easy going and light and they talked about everything from food to sex with no topic being off-limits. For instance, in the moment, Alexis made some cute comments about Tobias' accent and how she couldn't keep her hands off of him. Which caused Tobias to blush more than he intended.

Feeling the wine, Dasher on the other hand made sure that one part of her body was touching Mason at all times. He thought it was cute, but he thought she was cuter.

And then something happened.

A realization of sorts.

Right before they were preparing to ask for the check, Dasher laughed hard and heavily. And it was at that time that Mason saw that she not only resembled Banks before he transitioned, but that they were so similar it was startling.

And as she continued to talk and laugh, his gaze remained on her steadily. It was like he was transferred back in time, and he felt bad for thinking about another person at that moment.

"There you go staring at me again." Dasher said playfully, while rubbing his leg, lovingly. It was obvious she liked him, and he was feeling her too.

He whispered, "I think you're beautiful." He sat back in his chair and allowed his words to sink in. "So, I'm gonna stare. Consider it a good look."

She blushed. "Wow, that's the first time you complimented me seriously. I was starting to believe I wasn't your type."

"Go, head with that shit. I know you get compliments a lot." He sipped his drink.

"Sometimes." She shrugged. "But it doesn't matter if it's not from the right person. I mean, I'm sure you get plenty compliments too."

"Nah, I don't. I'm usually the one who gets insults."

She laughed again, and he stared harder. She was so fucking pretty. And the laugh was intoxicating.

"Well maybe your luck is about to change, mister. For the better."

"Talk your shit."

An hour later they were walking into the Louisville estate. The moment the foursome crossed the threshold Derrick rushed up to Mason with Shay following like bill collectors looking to get paid.

As was the common theme lately, it irritated him beyond belief that Mason was getting closer to Tobias. Their relationship had bonded so hard that when Mason wasn't with the twins, he was with Tobias.

But Derrick felt the duo strange as fuck.

"What you doing, pops? Did you know that mom lives with Banks while you out here running around town?"

Mason instructed Tobias and the ladies to go to the bar. When they were gone, he addressed his son. "Your mother gonna do what she gonna do. I'm not about to stop her no more."

"So, you get another woman instead?" He yelled.

"You not a kid. Your parents are separated. Grow the fuck up."

Derrick glared. "I can't believe you're actually fine with her being with your best friend. You must not have loved her."

"That's not what I said."

"Then how come it seems like you don't give a fuck? Huh? Tell me that!"

Mason considered his son a bit longer. "What is this *really* about?"

"It ain't about nothing but mom living with your best friend like she a whore. I mean, I thought when I told you she was with him, that you would bring her home. So, we can be a family. My clothes and shit ain't been cleaned in months."

"Derrick—."

"I'm serious!"

"You a grown fucking man!"

"I'm still your son!"

Mason took a deep breath. He had a female in the house and wanted to continue the wonderful evening he was having before entering the estate. Nowhere in the equation was he trying to spare the feelings of a grown man.

"Derrick, let me handle what I got in the back." He looked at Shay. "You handle yours." He focused back on Derrick and walked away.

"I don't like this relationship they building." She said.

"Well you shoulda said something. And clean the fucking house! You lazy as a two-day old baby."

"I don't think you want me to say what's on my mind. You may not be able to handle it." She looked at him once more and stormed away.

CHAPTER TEN

Winter was approaching because its cousin, fall, was in town.

Minnesota couldn't believe the luxury she was experiencing in the moment as she shared some wood with Myrio, which was their past time on the way to her surprise. There was no mistaking the fact that she came from money, but Myrio had gone all out to show her he knew how to spend heavily.

But why?

To celebrate her early birthday, the first thing he did was order a couple's massage at a spa in Virginia that was set up as if they were on an island.

After smoking again, they sat inside a never-ending pool overlooking the highway and drank mimosas while enjoying a catered lunch. He thought of every detail in an effort to make her feel special. Even took her to a five-star restaurant later in the evening, which he rented out so they could be alone.

Later on, that night he drove her to a friend's house, and she was excited all over again.

The moment they approached the home, she knew who ever lived there had a similar lifestyle to the one she had at Wales Mansion. Suddenly she felt at home. The person who was throwing the party was named Z, and that was all the information Myrio would provide.

Walking past the large pillars on the porch, when they stepped through the doubled doors, Minnesota grabbed his hand. "When we get inside, don't go too far. I don't know these people."

"Wherever you are I got my eyes on you. Trust me." He kissed her cheek. "You gonna be good."

The doors opened and they were immediately bombarded by smooth rap music and that quickly he disappeared like smoke in the open air.

She wasn't alone long.

Within one minute a short white girl with ginger hair stepped up to her with a huge smile on her face. Extending her fingertips that were dressed in silver glitter, she said, "You must be Minnesota."

Minnesota frowned and shook her hand.

The last thing she liked was people knowing her brand before she knew theirs. "Do I know you?"

"No but I feel like I've known you all my life."

"How?"

"Myrio talks about you all the time."

She crossed her arms over her chest. "Well what did he say?"

"Let's just say he wasn't wrong." Her eyes roamed on every area of Minnesota's body.

She felt somewhat relieved because he was apparently saying nice things. "Well, who are you? What is your name?"

"I'm a friend. That's all you need to know for now."

Minnesota dropped her arms. "Well I don't know how I feel about people knowing me without it being mutual. So, I would prefer some more information if you don't mind."

"I do mind actually." She touched her hand and squeezed lightly. "But I'll see you around." She winked. "I'm sure." She walked away.

What the fuck was that? She thought.

A few minutes later another girl switched over to her. She was a chocolate beauty with bohemian loc's that flowed effortlessly over her shoulders. "Hello, Minnesota. I'm Jasmine."

Minnesota was relieved that at least she seemed friendly enough to give a name. But the other chick appeared cool at first too and turned out strange. "It's nice to meet you."

"So, are you enjoying yourself so far? I told Myrio you'll be fine as he works the crowd. Most people here are nice."

"*Most*?"

"There's something strange in every crowd, right?"

She nodded in agreement as she looked from where she stood for the creeps. “Yeah, that’s probably why I’m a homebody these days. Meeting a bunch of new people at once is like a culture shock for me.”

“I can’t tell you’re shy. You look social enough.”

“I am kinda, when I’m amongst my own friends and amongst my own things.” Minnesota clarified.

“I get you.”

Minnesota could care less if she did or didn’t. “Thank you I guess.”

“But sometimes you have to get out of the house. Like when you were a kid going to school. Anybody can teach you how to read. But the whole purpose of schooling is to socialize you. Otherwise you can get left behind and become a monster. Do you know any monsters, Minnesota?”

She frowned. “No.” She was lying.

She knew many.

“Good, you are the great Minnesota Wales. And the world needs to know who you are before it bends to your power. Get out more. That’s my advice.”

This was getting weirder by the second hand clicking.

She was ready to bounce.

Minnesota glanced and looked around for Myrio and at the moment she didn’t spot him. So, she focused on the woman before her instead to pass the time. "Who are you with?"

Jasmine smiled. "You'll know when the time is right." She walked away.

After that encounter, Minnesota had enough. Finally spotting her date, she ran over to where Myrio was talking to another man and grabbed his hand. "I'm not feeling this place. Let's go."

He pulled away. "I'll get up with you later," he told his friend who walked off. Focusing on Minnesota he said, "We just got here."

"Correction we've been here for over an hour." She looked at her gold diamond Rolex. "And in that time, several bitches walked up to me on some strange shit. You wanna tell me what the fuck is going on? We started out having a nice day but—"

"You right, it did start out as a nice day so don't ruin it!"

She stepped back in awe.

Since they had been kicking it, he never talked to her in that manner. She was about to reply until he received a text message. Throwing up a finger, he checked it quickly and from her point of view, she glanced down and saw a woman named Erica.

She immediately grew heated. "You know what, this so stupid. I should have never given you a chance. You can take your little leased car back too."

She hoped he wouldn't want it back. She already ordered new wheels.

He tucked his phone in his pocket and smiled. "Jealous much?"

"Never that."

"That's not how you acting. It's a weird flex if you ask me."

"It's not a flex. I—"

"Look, I'm a popular guy. And you a popular woman. But my popularity stems from how I get money in these streets. You got your fame from hood royalty. And sometimes royals believe everybody supposed to drop everything for them. But that's not me."

"Myrio, you act like there's something wrong with me asking questions about these bitches who know my name."

"When did I say that?"

"You didn't say it. I'm judging by how you're acting."

"Listen, I think you fine as fuck."

"Myrio—"

"No, listen. Like I said, I think you fine. I really do. But that's all we got going with each other right now. When I invited you out, I said you should trust me."

"I know—"

"You fucked that up for me. Step off. You're Uber will be out front."

CHAPTER ELEVEN

This was the wettest Jersey had ever been and it felt fucking good. Banks didn't have any complaints either. Having her up under his body again reminded him of why they connected. Since she returned to him, they didn't have a fuck session unless they could look into each other's eyes.

The rhythm.

The moaning.

And even their body chemistry turned them both on. But when the sex was over, and he held her in his arms his mind wandered again.

While her thoughts projected to the past. Because although she was relieved to be home, he didn't seem to care about what she'd gone through under Mason's care. He was too infatuated that Mason hadn't made a move.

Had he really gotten over them being together?

Rolling over to face her, he looked into her eyes. "What you think he over there doing now?"

She frowned. "We just finished making love and that's what you ask me?"

"You think he plotting?"

She sighed. "You really want to know what I think, Banks? Or is this just another one of your setups? Because if you're really asking, I do have an opinion or two."

"I wanna hear what you think."

"I think it's very possible that he moved on. That he's not worried or concerned about us being together anymore."

Banks readjusted a little and laid on his back face up. One hand behind his head the other on his stomach as he thought about what she said.

It was his signature pose.

"No, I just, I just don't believe it."

"But why?" She yelled in frustration.

Her voice may have raised but it didn't rattle him in the least. He needed to solve the mystery. Since he'd been knowing Mason nothing about him was capable of letting go. He was a fighter. Always wanted the drama.

Always wanted the *war.*

"But why would he let us be together?" He looked at her. "He claimed you loved him so much. Even called you a loyal dog. And now he not gonna fight for you?"

Jersey sat on the edge of the bed. "Is it me or do you seem more concerned with him not wanting to fight over me, versus us being together?"

"Fuck that supposed to mean?"

She shrugged. "I'm just saying that the man appeared to have moved on. And yet you aren't happy with that. I don't get it. He's leaving us be. He's letting us go on with our lives. Maybe we should be grateful for his mercy."

"Fuck his mercy. I'm not feeling it." He ran his hand down his face as his temples, which hurt repeatedly, began to rock again. "Where are the twins?"

"You know where they are."

"I do, but I wanna hear you say the words."

"They're with Mason. It's his day to have them. I asked you about it yesterday and you agreed."

"That's what I'm talking about!" He sat on the edge of the bed having identified the conspiracy in his mind. "You and I had those babies. They ours! And yet he acting like he got two baby mamas over this bitch."

"Banks, stop!"

"I'm serious! Why does he get to have days for a family he Deebo'd himself into? Nobody invited him into our scenario, baby. You should be mad with me."

"So, what you wanna do? Tell him not to be involved? Because I'm not sure but I think he'll grant your wish if you ask."

He squinted. "So, you saying if I went to Mason and said we no longer want him in the picture with the twins, he would walk away?"

"Yes, Banks. I'm really starting to think he'll let go. When I dropped them off, he didn't seem the same. Something's different. And I like it."

It was almost leather jacket weather and Banks was handling business on the streets. Although touching the product was below him, because he liked to have his hands clean, he did reserve the right to check up on his lieutenants from time to time.

So far, everything looked good.

It appeared there was no drama when it came to business.

But what about other areas in his world?

His personal life was in turmoil and it gave him pain at night.

He was just about to head home when he got a call from one of Mason's men. As far as he knew he was a good dude who prided himself on building a strong team and making sure the count was right.

But what did he want with him?

"What up, William?" He turned left to merge onto the highway. "I'm busy."

"Sorry to bother you, sir. But have you talked to Mason?"

Banks' heart thumped and he pulled over on the side of the road to catch a calm rhythm. "No, is something wrong?"

"Not sure. It's just that I haven't seen him all day. He ain't answering calls either. Sometimes he stops by in the morning and sometimes it's at night. I mean, it's probably fine. I just didn't wanna miss him that's all. But I'll follow up later. Maybe he's—."

Relieved, Banks merged back on the road to turn in the opposite direction. "Nah, I'll go see if I can find him at home." Banks interrupted.

"No, sir! I don't want you to have to worry about that! I'll look for—."

"I said I got it!"

"But sir, those are the kinds of things we handle."

"And still you called me first. Like I said it's not a problem."

With a reason for a pop up in tow, an hour later Banks was in Mason's foyer at the Louisville estate. When he stepped inside, he saw him lovingly playing with the twins who were in double swings laughing at him as he made baby noises.

When Mason felt Banks' presence, he stood up and looked him over. "Everything good? You sounded anxious over the phone."

"William looking for you."

"Oh, yeah." He snapped his fingers and pointed. "I was supposed to collect the money today. But I wanted to spend time with the boys."

Banks thought about what Jersey said. If Banks told him he didn't want him in the twin's lives, would he do something to hurt Jersey or the kids? Or would he really let go?

"So, you don't work no more?" Banks crossed his arms over his chest. "I mean, I know you doing all this baby shit but there's money to be made too."

"Excuse me?"

"You heard me. You got people hitting my phone wondering where you are. You about the money or not?"

Mason shook his head as if he was tired of arguing. And in all the years of Banks knowing Mason, he had never seen him in such a way.

"Banks, is this about the boys? Do you want me out of their lives?"

Banks wasn't sure but there was something about his tone that led him to believe that Jersey was right. He was more than confident that if he said he wanted him out of the picture, that Mason would walk away.

Here was his chance.

"Banks, do you want me out of their lives or not?"

"I'm just trying to figure out if you still about the money."

He didn't take his exit.

Before Mason could respond, Tobias walked up. He shook Banks' hand. "Everything good, sir? Did you need anything from me?"

Banks' jaw twitched.

It was at that time that he could tell they were *close.*

Like *best friends.*

Like how they used to be.

And now, looking at Mason with a more concerning eye, it was evident that he wasn't defeated. He appeared lighter. Easier going. Stress free. Even his skin was clearer. At that moment, a ball of anger mixed with jealousy swished around the pit of his stomach.

But why?

The feeling was too strong to analyze. So, it progressed in a swirl of questions instead.

Why did Mason get to be at ease?

Why was he apparently happier?

More than it all, *why did he seem drama free when Banks was forced to put up with the nigga's shit for years?*

"No, I don't need anything else," Banks said to Tobias.

"Good, because me and Tobias on the way out." Mason replied. "Gina coming over to get the kids and I'll check William for my money later."

Banks nodded. "Good."

"Anything else, man?" Mason asked, shocked he was still there.

"Nah, I'ma chill with the boys until she gets here."

"You sure? Shay is—"

"I'm sure."

Mason nodded as he and Tobias walked toward the door, talking happily all the way.

Confused, and sick, Banks flopped on the sofa having realized one fate. That Mason Louisville, the man who hounded him for attention since they were kids, had officially let go.

Derrick was asleep until he sat up in bed, only to see his mother in his room placing clean underwear in his drawers. Since he wasn't wearing any because Shay was a horrible housekeeper, he covered his body with his dirty sheet, caked with nut and food.

Looking back, he was relieved to see his girl wasn't in the bed. "Ma, what you doing here? Why you ain't call?"

"Are you serious? You didn't have any clean underwear."

"Okay, well that's not your job no more. Unless you're back home. Are you home?"

"No."

He pouted like a big kid. "Then where are you staying?"

"At a hotel."

He glared. "I don't believe you."

She closed the drawer and sat on the edge of the bed. "Derrick—"

His eyes widened as if she was trying to suck his dick. "I said I don't have any underwear on, ma. Get up!"

"I'm your mother." She took a deep breath. "Listen, I want to say I understand why you told your father about me and Banks having the babies." She touched his leg.

"Ma, I don't have any clothes on!" He repeated. "Stop touching me."

"Derrick, I gave birth to you. I've seen it already." She sighed. "But I'm here because I don't want this for us. We're family and until I find Howard, we—."

He laughed.

"What's funny?" She asked.

"You have no idea, do you?"

"No idea about what?"

"Banks killed my brother a long time ago."

She stood up. "Who told you that?"

"Nobody. I can't prove it, but I feel it in my heart. I mean, ya'll did find Bet in Howard's freezer. It seems logical enough to me that he would kill him. And the moment I get proof, I'm taking your little boyfriend out myself. Without a word. You can count on that."

CHAPTER TWELVE

The heat blasted in Spacey's truck as the weather had become cooler. "I hear what you saying, but it's not like that. I just wanna settle down with someone I'm feeling in the moment." Spacey said to Joey as they drove down the street.

Every now and again he would look over at his brother's battered face, although he refrained from asking details on what happened because Joey was sensitive these days.

"Can't you do that while you date her? And just have fun." He leaned back into the seat. "Just don't see why marriage is the standard anymore. Look what happened to ma and pop."

Spacey nodded. "I could post up and play house." He shrugged. "Been doing that for months for real. I barely be home. But that's not how we are. We were raised in a two-parent home. And I like stability."

"We were a lot of things, but I don't know about stable." He sighed.

"Where your trucks?"

"At the shop."

Spacey didn't believe him. "So, uh, you talk to Minnesota?" He shifted a little. "She finally fucking with Tobias?"

"Nah, they seem to be on they different shit now. He spends a lot of time with Mason. Saw them at some restaurant awhile back with two females. Cute too. Especially the one Mason with."

"So, Tobias is really living in the house? Like nothing ever happened on Skull?"

"Is that the reason you moved out?" Spacey made a left.

"One of the reasons. The other is I don't trust him. When he was on that island, he was strange."

"He's actually cool. We need the money to keep flowing. And what better way to do that then play host to the plug's son?"

"After all this time, you still wanna be a drug dealer so bad."

"You sound stupid."

Joey laughed and quieted down a little. "So, dad still cool with Mason?"

"I'm not sure, but I don't think so. Something feels off."

"You mean besides him fucking Aunt Jersey?" Joey looked out the car window as his brother drove.

"Well Mason fucked ma too."

Joey nodded. "Do you ever think about ma and Harris?"

"All the time."

"It's like when they were around, shit was better. But you about to get married and I'm out here..."

Spacey looked over at him. "You out here what?"

Alone. He thought.

"Never mind." Joey replied.

"You got Minnesota. Ain't nobody marrying her. She'll be around."

"It ain't the same thing."

Spacey sighed. For some reason Joey felt heavy and he didn't know why. "You think she would've liked my fiancé? I'm talking about ma."

"Why you asking me that? Because she a big girl?"

"You always gotta say stupid shit?"

"You know I'm just fucking around." Joey looked out the window and suddenly his eyes opened wide. Popping up, he pointed a stiff finger into the glass leaving behind greasy fingerprints with each peck. "Pull over up there right quick!"

"For what?"

"Just do it, man." He unbuckled his seat belt and leaned to open the door before it stopped. "I have something I gotta check on."

"But I gotta pick up some—."

"Just pull over!" He yelled. "Please." He said softer.

Since he said it nicer, Spacey pulled over although he wasn't happy about it one bit. "Whatever you about to do, make it quick."

"Okay!" Joey bolted out of the truck and ran back to the house he spotted before Spacey changed his mind.

Annoyed, Spacey slowly backed up until he parked in front of the house he disappeared into. It was a nice enough row home. Wasn't too much going on outside and it looked like an okay neighborhood for kids.

So why did he feel strange?

"What is this nigga up to?" He said to himself.

While texting his fiancé, he listened to the radio and thought about how within a matter of weeks he would be a married man. He liked the idea of having a wife too. Of having a woman who would take care of his every need. But Spacey had some dark ideas and concepts he didn't tell many people about.

Ten minutes later a white Honda pulled up behind him and parked. Within seconds, three people, two men and one woman, piled out of the car. Moving strangely, they looked at Spacey and entered the house.

What was going on?

Concerned, he readjusted in his seat and attempted to squint through the window to get a better view.

It didn't work.

After a while, two people he never saw enter, exited. Three women. They all looked dingy and one wasn't wearing shoes. None of them looked like they showered in weeks.

Spacey texted Joey a few times.

Aye...where u at? Its creepy AF out here.

He didn't answer.

Curious, he exited his car and knocked on the door. When no one answered he peered through the front window. Now he could see clearly. What he witnessed caused him to shiver. There in the living room, was his brother, sitting on the sofa with a needle in his arm. He was lying back, mouth wide open.

Nodding.

With his heart thumping, Spacey had all intentions on kicking the door down. But he decided to turn the knob first.

It clicked open.

Aware of his surroundings, he walked inside and shoved past a few men sitting on the floor. All had sinister looks on their faces, but all appeared to be addicts too.

Grabbing his brother, he literally carried him to the car and pulled off.

An hour later they were in the parking lot of a grocery store. Spacey was on the outside, leaning against the side smoking a cigarette, trying to process what happened with his kid brother. While Joey was inside head still wobbling as he came down from his high.

After five more minutes Spacey opened the door and slid inside the driver seat. Throwing his hands up he said, "What are you doing, Joey? What the fuck are you doing, man? I don't get it. Is this why your face is fucked up? Did you steal from somebody and get whooped?"

Joey rubbed his temples. "Leave me alone, Spacey."

"So, you a fucking addict now? That's how you going down?"

"I'm not an addict. I just do a little something to tide me over every now and again."

"So, heroin tides you over?"

"Heroine, coke, weed, to be honest I don't care half the time what I'm taking." He shook his head. "I just need, I just want the thoughts to go away every now and again. But don't go tripping and telling pops crazy shit. It's the last thing I need right now."

Spacey was hurt but above all he was embarrassed for his sibling. "I'm not understanding." He threw his hands up. "Why, man? Can you at least tell me that?"

Joey flopped back in his seat and looked up at the roof. "Do you think it's my fault that ma...never mind."

"Say it. Why are you on drugs?"

"After everything that happened to us you really asking me that question?"

"You saying this because of ma and Harris?"

"What else?"

"Nigga, stop making excuses. We all fucked up out here."

"It's not about making excuses. It's about the truth. I don't feel like thinking about all of this right now anyway. I don't feel like thinking about none of it. So, I'm trying to handle things the best I can."

He could hear he was ready to play the victim. "If this is going to be you, I don't want you around me." He pointed in his face. "That's all I'm gonna say."

"So, we not brothers no more?" Joey laughed. "That's how you going out?"

Spacey shook his head and drove him home.

Two hours later Spacey was at his girlfriend's house. She made dinner which included fried chicken, mashed potatoes and broccoli for her man. While she herself feasted on a large salad.

Over dinner they had light conversation with wine, but he was zeroed in on her closely. Like a crossword puzzle. There were certain things he enjoyed about her. Certain things that weren't up for negotiation, and that included losing weight.

So why did she look thinner?

"So, my co-worker said she was going to fuck him but—."

"What you doing?" He asked, cutting her off. "What is all this?"

She frowned. "What you talking about?"

He looked at her plate. "Lately you've been eating light." He wiped his mouth with the linen napkin and tossed it on the table. "And I wanna know why. Because you look the fuck terrible."

She shuffled a little and sat her fork down. "If I am losing weight, what's the problem?"

He glared. "Where you wanna start?"

She sat back. "Spacey, don't start an argument. Not again. I wanted, I mean, I wanted this to be a good night."

He leaned into the table. "Let me make myself clear. I had a long day. You know I'm a drug lord. In charge of a lot of shit and a lot of people."

A drug lord? She thought.

Instead she nodded. "Of course, I do."

"A lot of niggas depend on me. More than my father. Bolero himself, depends on me. If I'm not right in the head, shit falls."

"Honey, I understand."

"Do you? Because after what I learned today, about my brother, my days may be fucked up for a while. The last thing I want is my fiancé to look different than the woman I fell for. Big, thick and pretty is my thing."

"Spacey—."

"You like this house?" He looked around.

Her eyes widened. "Yes, of course I do. I—."

"You lose one pound, just one, and I'ma throw you the fuck out of it."

He grabbed her plate and piled it high with what he was eating. When he was done, he slid it over to her. “Now eat. Every fucking bit.”

Slowly she picked up the fork, as it shook in her hand, and finished the large meal.

After a long day, Tobias walked into his room, preparing to go to bed. But when he turned the light on, he noticed Spacey sitting on his mattress as if he were a whore he paid for.

“Spacey, what you doing in here?” He jumped. “I thought you moved with your fiancé?”

“Can I talk to you for a minute?”

He frowned. “About what? I wanted to get some sleep. Me and Mason just came from the club and—”

“What do you do when your girl ain’t acting right?”

He ran his hand down his face and sighed. Leaning up against the door he said, “What exactly is going on again?”

“It’s like, I like her how she is and she’s trying to change on me. Why do women do that? When we think they perfect as they are?”

“Spacey, I have a long day in front of me. Can we talk about this later? Please?”

Spacey stared at him a minute longer, got up and hugged him. It was a long embrace that was strange and awkward.

“You do that, man. We’ll get up later.” He tapped him on the shoulder and walked out.

CHAPTER THIRTEEN

Mason was in his mansion inside of his bedroom hitting his girlfriend's pussy from the back. Her moans were soft and delicate, and her body was as warm as a recently turned off oven. Whenever he thrust deeper into her, she pushed back catching him blow for blow.

When he felt himself about to reach a premature ejaculation, he flipped her over, spread her legs and eased into her again. She was slippery and ready.

Wanting his body next to hers she snaked her arms around his back and pulled with all of her strength forcing his muscular chest into the softness of her breasts.

As he looked down at her face he was in a trance.

To say she resembled Blakeslee would be an understatement. What was odd was the way her eyes met his, they connected on a level reserved for soul mates.

"Mason, you, you feel so good." She moaned. "Please don't stop, baby. Please, please don't stop making love to me."

He grabbed her legs allowing each to fall over his shoulders like a scarf. Kissing the flesh of her inner thigh, he pressed deeper and deeper until he could go no further. Up until that point she thought she had received him fully.

She was wrong.

"Fuck, I'm cuming." He announced. "This shit feels so, so fucking good. Why your pussy this wet huh?"

"Cum inside me, Mason. I wanna feel you. Please."

He pushed and pushed more and when he felt himself exploding, he yelled, "Blakeslee, I'm, I'm almost there! Shitttttt!"

It was a powerful orgasm that almost hurt because it felt so good.

Having reached goal, he fell into her body and pushed harder, until every ounce of his nut was deposited inside of her as if her pussy was the bank. When they were done, she laid on her side and he eased behind her. Kissing her on the back of her shoulder, he inhaled the scent of her body.

"Who is Blakeslee?" She asked.

Fuck, he hoped she hadn't heard his mistake.

"The love of my life."

She sighed. "Do you, I mean, do you love her still?"

"I'll love her for the rest of my life."

"Is that who you see when you look at me?"

"Yes."

She nodded. "You know, I always felt something. I mean, when you stare at me, it's like I feel her presence. It's like I'm her." She wiped her hair behind her ear. "I knew it was impossible for a man to be so intense without a reason. Whoever she is, she's a lucky woman to have your heart."

"She's dead."

She smiled in relief.

She experienced what it felt like to compete with ghosts in the past so finding out Blakeslee was gone was all she needed to know. "In that case you can call me her name." She smiled brighter. "It's a nice name. I won't mind. Just as long as you stay."

Mason was driving down the road on the way to meet Tobias. He left his girl at his house because she was fast asleep and at the end of the day, he liked her in his bed.

Waiting on dick.

There were many things on his mind. Things he wouldn't tell another soul. Arlyndo's death was still heavy on his heart. He would be there had he been smarter. Besides, had he listened to Banks on the island and not drank tainted sangria, he would possibly still be alive.

And then he thought about Patterson. And how because of his own actions against Howard, he was killed by his own brother.

When he made it to the parking lot to meet Tobias for his money, once again he caught him meditating in the car with his eyes closed. Knocking on the window lightly Tobias smiled and unlocked the door.

Mason slid inside.

"You know I could've come to the house, right?" Tobias said.

"Yeah, but I needed the drive." He grabbed the money bag. "For some reason, lately I been going through it mentally. I haven't gotten over...losing Arlyndo, Patterson and not knowing where Howard is. And this shit with Jersey. Plus..." Mason grew quiet.

"Plus, what?"

"The worst part is Banks..."

Tobias nodded.

"I don't like where we are but, I'm done with it all."

"Maybe you should talk to him."

"Nah, I actually like not worrying about if he good. If we gonna be good. Always being on edge is like a constant fire. And sometimes the flames get so high I have to react. Usually when it happens shit gets violent." He looked at Tobias. "Can meditation help with that?"

"Maybe, but it won't be easy. The hardest thing for a man to do is sit with his own thoughts. You never think about how difficult it is until you try. Most people say, *'Of course, I can do it. I'll just have to sit down and be quiet for ten minutes.'* But inside of silence is every demon you've entertained begging for attention. Trying to stop you from having peace of mind."

"So, who the fuck would wanna go through all that?"

"Everybody if you knew what was on the other side." He said excitedly. "Because, because there's another level. Once you surpass it, every thought, and everything you fear disappears. You realize it doesn't matter. And you become free."

"I still don't get it."

"It's hard to explain but once you can sit with yourself, flaws and all, you become untouchable."

It sounded fluffy to Mason, but he was desperate for a change. So, with a deep breath he said, "Okay, teach me that shit."

Banks was in a dark place.

The darkest place he'd ever been and that was heavy considering everything he'd gone through.

As he stood next to his truck watching Mason and Tobias inside of the car, his blood ran cold. In reality they were meditating. But Banks' mind saw something else. Two men on the verge of falling in love. He was so sick with rage, that his vision blurred.

And yet, he couldn't identify the source of his anger.

After all, Mason was compliant in Banks' every desire. He wanted him to stop causing problems, so Mason stepped back. He wanted Jersey so Mason let her go. And above all, Banks said he wanted to be left alone.

And again, Mason granted his wish.

So where was the dilemma?

Why wasn't Banks Wales finally at peace?

An hour later Banks was in the twins' Nursery. They were always so happy and excited to see him, and it made him smile, especially Ace.

Walid was another story. He seemed quieter and more reserved, and Banks noticed his disposition was different at all times.

Creepy even.

He was still playing with them when the door opened, and Jersey walked into the room. "I didn't know you were home."

He took a deep breath. "Yeah, just wanted to spend some time with the boys before they go to sleep."

"Gina has them on a good schedule." She rubbed his shoulder. "Well, I made dinner. I waited for you but it's in the microwave."

"Did Minnesota eat?"

"She hasn't been here in a while. Neither has Spacey or Joey. Something strange is going on in the house. You hungry?"

"Nah."

She moved uneasily. "Banks, I wanna ask you something."

He looked at her.

"Did you, did you kill my son?"

He frowned having known the moment would come. "Why would you ask me something like that?"

"I, I've been trying to find him. I've been trying to, trying to understand what was going on between him and Bet. And I can't wrap my mind around it."

"Do you like it here? With me?"

"Yes, of course I do."

"Then never ask me something like that again. The next time there won't be an argument. There won't be a reconnect. We'll be over."

This hit her like a heavyweight fighter's fist to the gut.

His answer was enough.

It had to be.

Nodding, she sat next to him on the floor and playfully touched Walid's foot. For a baby, he appeared to stare at her intensely as if he'd been here before. "They're getting so big. And so healthy."

Banks nodded. "Doesn't Walid look like Mason?"

She shrugged. "Kinda, I guess."

"Look closer. They legit have the same features. It's crazy."

She looked at Banks a little and then focused on the babies. Something was strange. "You don't seem to hate the idea of Mason being the father anymore. Why is that?"

"Who said he was the father?"

"You know what I mean."

"Then what you saying?"

"Banks, stop trying to fight with me. I'm just asking if you mind Mason being in the picture anymore?"

Banks stood up and sat on the sofa within the nursery. "I haven't thought about it much." He lied. "To tell you the truth I haven't thought about Mason either."

She walked over to him and sat on his lap. They were face to face. Looking down at him she said, "Now you and I both know that ain't true. Since when did we get to that place? Where we, where we aren't honest with each other?"

"You want me to say something I don't feel?"

"Of course not. You and I are better than that. I just wanna know, I mean, why does Mason's distance appear to be a problem all of a sudden? It's like you miss him more than me."

Banks laughed hard. "Do you realize how crazy you sound?"

"No, because I don't think I'm wrong."

"I'm not checking for that nigga. If he's gone, good riddance."

"If you say so."

She leaned in for a kiss, but he shoved her lightly. "I'm serious. I'm glad he's giving us our distance. I just don't trust his reasons that's all."

"I'm sick of talking about him. What's up with us?"

She unzipped his pants and pushed him back on the sofa. Sitting on his lap she removed his stick and placed it into her body. By now she knew how to work her hips to give him the right sensation by keeping it in the right place. Besides, he always wore his dick as if it were an extension of him.

"I love you, and that's all I care about," she said softly.

He grabbed her hips and maneuvered her the way he liked. In that moment, neither said a word. It was all about Jersey and Banks.

So why was his mind on Mason?

Banks was in the warehouse going over the recent shipment Bolero delivered. A few of his men outlined the perimeter per usual to make sure no one tried anything risky. Within ten minutes, Mason came rushing through the door U.S. military style, followed by five of his men.

The moment he saw Banks' face he felt relieved.

Looking around quickly he tucked his weapon in the back of his pants and stormed up to him. "What happened, are you okay? You been hit?" He eyed his body.

Banks whispered in one of the men's ear who was packaging. "Everyone out!" Banks' packager yelled. All of the workers left, leaving Mason, Banks and Mason's men alone.

Banks walked up to him. "Took you long enough."

Mason was confused and frowned. "Fuck you mean? You said to come right away and that it was urgent. I was here in less than five minutes. Did something pop off?" He looked around from where he stood. All was in order.

"What's up with you and Tobias?"

Mason frowned. "What you talking about?"

"I think I made myself clear. Ya'll been keeping a lot of time. A bit strange if you ask me."

Mason dragged his hands down his face. He looked back at his men. "Leave us alone."

"You sure?" One soldier asked Mason.

Banks glared at him.

Mason nodded and the men exited.

Turning around to Banks Mason said, "I'm confused. Did somebody try to break in the warehouse or not?"

"If you would've hit me back, I wouldn't have done this. Now, I asked you a question. Still waiting on an answer."

"Not for nothing, brother, but my dealings with Tobias ain't none of your concern. I don't question you on your friends. Why you questioning me about mine?"

The fact that he kept calling him *brother* rang to Banks as weird. "So now you're friends with Bolero's son? Is it me or does that seem off?"

"It's off if you make it that way. I see it as good business."

Banks looked down and back up. "How do I know I can trust you, Mason?"

He laughed. "If you haven't trusted me before why should you start now? As a matter of fact, I can't think of any time, *ever*, where you trusted me to be honest. So, can I go now? I got shit to do later."

Banks lowered his brow. "So, it's like that? You dipping out when I'm trying to speak?"

"What am I doing wrong now, brother?" He threw his arms up. "I've given you everything you asked. You wanted my wife; I gave her to you! You wanted peace I let you have that. You wanted me out your life, I stepped the fuck off! Why you doing all of this now? Help me understand because for real, I'm lost."

Silence.

When Banks refused to respond, Mason stepped closer. "Did somebody try to get in the warehouse tonight? Or was that all a ploy to get me here?"

Silence.

"I don't know what's going on with you, brother. But whatever it is, I'm not feeling it."

Banks smiled sinisterly. "Calling me *brother* won't change how you feel about me. But if it works, you do what you do."

"Meaning?"

Silence.

Having gotten his answer, and believing Banks was salty, Mason shook his head, smiled and walked out, leaving Banks alone.

Mason was driving down the street after meeting with Banks when his phone rang. "What?"

"Mason."

When he heard the voice, he looked at the phone with disgust before putting it back on his ear. "What do you want, Jersey?"

"My son. Where is he?"

Mason sighed deeply. “I really don’t know. But trust me, I’ve been looking for him everywhere.”

“Well, Derrick had some wild ideas about what may have happened. And I want you to know whatever he says, it’s not true.”

“Well what did he say?”

Silence.

“Jersey, what did he say?”

“He said Banks was involved.”

Mason frowned. “Nah, that would never happen.”

“I said the same thing. Just—.”

“Aye, Jersey.” He interrupted her.

“Yes?”

“Never hit my phone again. You ain’t mine no more. Remember? I don’t fuck with pass arounds.” He hung up.

CHAPTER FOURTEEN

Joey had a long day.

Unlike in the month's past, he had stayed over his father's house because the girl he was staying with decided to throw him out. Mainly because unlike in the days before, he no longer had money.

When Joey eased out of his old bed the rain poured harder against the house. It fit his mood perfectly.

Grim.

In fact, it was hurricane season and it seemed to be more gloomier days than were sunny ones.

Finally pushing himself out of the bed and getting into the shower, he thought about his life. An addict was not supposed to be a Wales member. After all, he came from royalty.

Hood royalty but royalty none the less.

After showering and getting dressed he walked into the foyer and then outside where a car awaited him. To be honest the plan for the day brought him great distress. Because for some reason, Banks asked him to help with the coke shipment, something he didn't do before.

Back in the day, prior to Bolero, he may have pushed around a few boxes here and there but that was the extent of his help. Joey's major fear was that he hoped he wouldn't fall victim to his urges.

It was horrifying.

After getting out of the car and going to the warehouse he was brought to the third floor of a huge building. The moment he was inside, Banks walked up to him. Two men stood behind his father and he felt strange.

"Son, is everything okay? You look uneasy."

Joey shuffled around a little. "Uh, yeah, dad. I'm surprised you asked for my help that's all." He whispered.

"Why wouldn't I?" Banks placed a heavy hand on his shoulder.

Joey tried to move from under his hold but was unsuccessful. He hadn't expected that question. "I don't know." He shrugged. "I just figured since I haven't been helping it was out of my realm of responsibility."

He removed his hand. "Well you never know when I'll ask for help. It's best to stay ready." He pointed behind Joey. "Come over here with me."

Within seconds, Joey was led to a part of the floor where cocaine piles sat on top of long tables. As he made the trek, there were women scattered about who were bagging vigorously. Unlike in the movies they were fully dressed. Wearing black stretch pants and tight camisole's so that if they stole anything their shapes would be altered.

"I need you to watch over them and make sure this bundle is packaged no later than..." Banks looked at his watch. "Forty minutes."

"Pops, I don't know about this."

He shrugged. "What's there to know?"

"I just don't feel comfortable."

"Son, I really need your help. Can you do this for me? I mean look at it this way. It's work. Get it done and you'll get paid." He placed a heavy hand on him again and walked away.

It was facts.

Joey definitely could use the money, so he relented and fifteen minutes later Joey was still watching over the women. He was doing well at first, and suddenly after being around so many drugs, he felt the pangs of addiction whisper into his ear. His body told his secret when his forehead began to sweat. His body began to tremble. He felt uneasy and unable to stay still.

Keep it together, Joey. He told himself.

It didn't work.

Finally succumbing to the urge, he walked towards one of the tables on some slick shit. At the furthest end where small packages were sitting. Since they were no bigger than his thumb, he grabbed one when no one was looking and tucked it in his waistline.

Within seconds, he was swarmed by Banks' men. Embarrassed, Joey's eyes widened, and he smiled awkwardly trying to pretend nothing was off. "What's going on, pops?"

Banks didn't provide an answer. He was hurt and devastated that one of his sons took this route. "What you doing?" He pulled the drugs out.

"Pops, I was just...I mean..."

Disgusted he said, "get him out of here."

Banks' devastation lasted so long that he remained silent as Joey was transported to another location like bulk trash. After some time, they arrived at a three-story Brick House in Landover Maryland.

When they were in front of the house, Banks along with his trusted men piled out of vehicles. Still, he refused to talk to his son.

"Pops, what's going on? Can you...can you tell me something?"

Again, Banks remained silent while Joey was ushered inside, through a living room, down a long hallway and into a bedroom in the back of a house. Once inside the smaller space, it quickly became evident that this would be home.

There was a bed on the floor. A TV. And a small table with water and sugar. Without an answer, he was thrown to the floor as Banks covered the doorway. "No son of mine will take this route in life."

"Pops, please don't do this to me. I, I was going through a lot and, and, I know I shouldn't have tried to steal, but you don't understand. Things have been hard on me. I'm not as strong as you are."

"I know. So, we're going to have to remedy that."

CHAPTER FIFTEEN

Dinner was served in the dining room inside of the Wales estate.

Although some were in the mood to eat and talk about the family's upcoming functions, others were annoyed. In attendance was Banks, Jersey, Minnesota, Spacey, his fiancé, Shay and Derrick by Jersey's request.

She claimed she wanted him involved.

When it was time to speak, Banks stood up from the table. "Before we begin let me be clear that tonight is not about past gripes. We are putting all negativity aside."

"I know what you're doing, dad." Minnesota said. "Trying to make me out to be the bad girl."

"I'm not doing anything. Just making it clear that we are here to discuss the wedding. And what responsibilities each of us will take. I've already made clear that this wedding is very important, and I want to see to it that things are carried out properly."

"Thank you, Pops," Spacey smiled. "Like I said when this first went down, we hadn't planned on doing anything big, so this is...it means a lot." He nodded. "Tobias will be here, too right?"

Banks glared. Why did he have to bring him up?

"I'm not sure. You gotta ask him."

Spacey frowned. "I really want him to be here."

Banks nodded. "I'll see what I can do."

"You are acting like such a female," Minnesota said to Spacey. "Begging for another man's attention and shit. Be happy with your fiancé."

Spacey glared. "You know, I had hopes that your selfishness would go away the older you got. For a while, you really fooled me into believing that you grew up. But now I'm seeing that portion of you won't go anywhere."

"You mean the portion of me that's tired of being overlooked?"

"Since when have you gone overlooked?" Spacey yelled slamming a fist down on the table. "Name one time. I'll wait." He crossed his arms.

She glared. "Don't go there with me."

"I'm serious. For the entire first portion of my life all that mattered was you. *What Minnesota wanted. What Minnesota needed.* That's not even talking about the fact that you started the war between Pops and Mason."

"Spacey, don't do that," Banks said.

"Seriously, dad. It was all her fault, and everyone knows it."

"When is everybody gonna let that shit go? It's weird how nobody minds telling me I'm young, but they love bringing up shit I did when I was a kid."

"It's easy for you to say let things go when you were the one who caused all the pain." Spacey continued. "I often wondered what might have happened if you and Arlyndo hadn't decided to betray pops. Ma and Harris would probably still be alive. Arlyndo too since we talking."

"Spacey, stop it!" Banks yelled. "I'm serious!"

Minnesota began to cry. "Their deaths were not my fault!"

"This dinner is going away from what we wanted tonight." Jersey said.

"You're right. But I think we do need to talk about this. The problem with some people is they believe if a thing is not said, then it doesn't matter anymore. But not me. Maybe we should finally get everything out on the table."

"Spacey, I would really prefer if we didn't bring up dark days." Jersey said.

"No offense, but a person who sleeps with her husband's best friend shouldn't be allowed to speak on much of anything." Derrick said.

Banks pointed at him. "I don't know what you do at the Louisville estate but around here you will not disrespect your mother."

"You're right, she's my mother, *Unc.* But I still have a big problem with your relationship!" He looked at Jersey, "and the fact that you had babies with him. Forcing pops to be the father."

"Wait, Mason is the father of the twins?" Minnesota asked, wiping her tears.

Banks was heated.

"Is that true?" Spacey asked.

"It's a long story." Banks said. "At the end of the day, yes. Mason involved himself into a situation that didn't concern him."

"Yet another reason why ya'll shouldn't be together," Derrick said. "He still loves you, ma. I know it."

"Derrick, I suggest you get over it." Jersey said. "Because I'm not leaving Banks for nothing in the world."

"I can't believe this shit." He said under his breath. "This is so embarrassing."

"What can't you believe?" Jersey said angrily. "You have spent so much time worrying about what I do and who I do it with that you're failing to live your own life. I want the best for you but not at my expense, son. Not anymore. And then you disrespect Banks in his house?"

"What about the disrespect to me? And Arlyndo? And Patterson? And Howard, wherever he is?" He looked at Banks. "Where is he, Unc?"

"I don't know what you talking about." Banks glared.

"I'm moving on with my life." Jersey interrupted. "And I want you to be a part of that. I need you to be a part of that. You have two brothers who are babies who would do well by—."

"Those things are not my brothers."

Banks knew he was hurting but his patience had thinned.

Jersey on the other hand was devastated. "You mean to tell me that you would disown your brothers? Who have nothing to do with being in this world?"

"I mean to tell you just that."

When Jersey began to cry, Banks was no longer interested in being cool and collected. "Let me be clear, Derrick! You will show respect in my house or you will never be welcomed back again. Your choice."

Derrick wanted to talk more but Shay squeezed his hand.

"Now your mother has made it clear that she wants you in her life. But wanting you in her life doesn't give you any reason to believe you will change what's going on between us. Get with it or get the fuck out." He pointed at the door.

"Whatever." Derrick shook his head but remained silent.

"Good, now let's eat."

Although difficult, later on that night they talked about the details of Spacey's wedding. But it was obvious that not everybody was on board.

After most of the details were hashed out, once again Banks went on a mental vacation. He even took to the whiskey bottle whole. Getting so drunk he went downstairs to think in peace.

After a while, he made a call. "Did you ever stay in contact with that girl?" Banks asked Mason. "The one you met who did the massages."

"You mean the cute white girl who lived in Delaware?"

Banks sat back on the sofa and sipped his whiskey straight from the bottle. "Yeah. Her."

"Nah, she was tripping a little, so I had to cut her off. And when she reached out again talking about giving me massages for the low, I was married and too busy by that time. She didn't work out."

"I always wondered if you stayed in contact. You seemed to be falling for her a little bit." Banks took a deep breath. "We were going over Spacey's wedding tonight."

"Oh yeah, shit good?"

"Not really. Derrick is...you know, mad."

"I can imagine how he feels."

Banks sighed and took another drink. "Look, I'm about to go to the bar. You wanna grab a drink or..."

"I can't, brother. I'm going out."

Banks readjusted in his seat. "W...where?"

"Me and Tobias going to this club. Did you—."

Banks hung up.

He was embarrassed that he called. Embarrassed that he reached out. And more than anything, he was embarrassed that he was rejected.

What he had to determine was what he was going to do with his rage.

Or who he was going to hurt.

CHAPTER SIXTEEN

When Tobias made it home, to the Wales estate, the plan was to get in bed and call it a night. After all, in addition to working with Bolero his days were filled with spending time with his new lady. And when he was not with her, he was with Mason talking about frivolous things.

Wanting to grab some whiskey, he was surprised to see Banks sitting by the fireplace drinking something dark in a crystal glass. "Oh, I'm sorry. I didn't know anyone was up this late."

Banks chuckled once. "Why not, I live here."

Tobias smiled. "I didn't mean it that way. Of course, this is your home."

"No reason to be sorry." Banks raised his glass. "Sit down and join me."

Tobias nodded, walked inside filled his glass and sat across from Banks in a leather recliner. Taking a sip, he laid back into the butter soft seat. "Sir, you always did have taste when it came to liquor."

"Thank you." He crossed his legs grown man style. Ankle to the knee. "So, talk to me, Tobias. Where have you been? What have you been up to these days?"

"Sir?"

"I mean, at one point I saw a lot of you around but lately you seem to come and go so easily."

"Just trying to find my place in the United States." He sighed and took a deeper sip. "I won't lie. At one point I was afraid I wasn't going to like it here but now...its cool. I'll just say that."

Banks nodded. "How is Rosa? And your sisters?"

"Sir, that's what I wanted to talk to you about. Things aren't going as well as I'd like with my sisters. They miss me. Especially Casandra. I guess they're growing and at odds with my mother too. So, Bolero has arranged for them to come here for a few weeks."

"Where they staying?"

"I'm not sure."

Banks nodded. "Sounds good. Hope it works out."

"Other than that, they're satisfied, I think. Mama likes the home you built. It's plenty of space inside where they don't see each other for days. Land that stretches far enough to plant plenty of fruit and vegetables."

"You don't have to tell me. I built it for my family remember? On the land I purchased from your father, although I didn't know at the time."

"I don't consider Bolero my father." He took another sip.

"Even still?"

"Yes. Because there was a period in our lives where we could have used the help. But he allowed us to believe that our real father was on the run before eventually landing in prison. But it was all because of his crimes. Not my uncle's. I don't have to tell you that it makes it hard for me to trust him."

"*Trust.*" Banks raised his glass. "Now that's a word."

"Why you say that?"

"Mainly because this generation throws the term around like dick. And so, it's hard to build a relationship on genuine trust these days. There are a lot of factors that come in play."

"I understand."

"Do you? Because you have to be with a person, you're on the verge of trusting through the storms. Through the hurricanes. And afterwards, if that person is still around despite it all, that's how you build a lasting bond. That's how you build, *trust.*"

"I'm sure you have a lot of people around you who fit the bill."

"Maybe. But I don't have a lot of people *I* trust around me."

"Sir, I want to be upfront with you about something. Something that's been on my mind."

"I'm listening." He took a sip.

"I don't think it will work with me and Minnesota. I wanted it to but it's really not in the stars for us."

He smiled. "I can't say I didn't see this coming. But let me hear it from you. What brought about the change?"

"I think she's attracted to Myrio. I think she's really trying to make something work with him. And I don't want to get in the way."

"She's young. And ambitious."

"I know. But so am I." He paused. "I might not be as young as Minnesota, but I do have my life ahead of me. And I want to spend those moments with people who want to be with me. I hope you understand."

"That's very admirable."

"Just trying to be honest."

"*Honesty.* Now that's another loosely thrown around word."

Tobias moved around a little because he was starting to realize something was up. Heart beating like a boom box, he placed his glass on the table next to him. "Sir, did I do something wrong?"

"Only you know the answer to that question."

"I'm confused. I assumed we were getting along fine here. Whenever you need me, I'm there."

"You are."

"So, if I overstepped my boundaries in any way please make it clear. I mean, is this about Minnesota? Because I refuse to disrespect you in anyway."

"If it had been about my daughter, this conversation would be one sided. With me standing over your grave. Let's agree on that."

Tobias glared and for the first time Banks could see Bolero's resemblance.

There the killer go. Banks thought.

"You know, I used to love watching Korean thriller movies." Banks continued skipping the subject. "I would spend hours trying to find the right one. When I got a good one, I would be focused. Not that they were hard to follow, but you had to be paying attention to get the key moments. With the language barrier, you turn around one second, and you could miss the whole point. And I turned around for one second with you. But I'm paying attention now."

Banks grabbed his phone and texted a number. Placing it face down on the end table he took a deep breath. And stared at him for what seemed like eternity.

"Sir, what's going on?"

Banks grabbed his glass, whirled the liquor around inside for a few moments and said, "You'll see."

Two minutes later everything Tobias possessed sat in expensive luggage at the doorway. "Sir, I'm really confused now. I mean, are you, are you throwing me out?"

"I wouldn't call it that, but I am giving you an opportunity to live your fullest life in this country. Away from me. Away from my inquisition's. Because at the end of the day to be *honest*, I don't *trust* you."

"Please don't do this. I have nowhere else to go."

"You're rich."

"All of my money goes home, sir. Every penny."

"I'm quite sure you'll figure it out." Banks looked at his men. "Make sure he gets off my property. Expeditiously." Banks rose and walked away.

CHAPTER SEVENTEEN

Mason was on his way to pick up his girlfriend Dasher from her hair appointment. Normally he wouldn't find time for girlish matters but after being on the verge of divorce and reassessing his life he realized he needed to put time into what mattered the most.

He was almost at the shop when he spotted a friend of Howard's. He pulled over, almost hitting a car in the process.

Although he was certain Howard moved on with his life in another part of the United States, he wanted nothing more than to speak to his son. And to let him know that if he returned, things would be okay.

Parking the car, he got out and walked up to Sam. "What you been up to?" Mason asked.

Horrified, Sam froze and looked around, to see if he came with hitters. "Uh, nothing. Is everything okay?"

His eyes were wide with fear and it put Mason off. "Not really. You been in contact with Howard?"

He frowned. "In contact?"

"Yes. I've been putting feelers out to see if anybody heard anything and I'm coming up short. I figured since you and he were close at one point—"

"I stopped dealing with Howard after he went *that way.*"

Mason shot daggers. "What way you talking about, son?"

"You know what I mean." He shrugged. "*That way.*"

Mason glared. And although he had been meditating for two to three minutes a day to get his mind right, after hearing the disrespect, his need for peace was replaced with his need for violence.

"Nigga, don't get killed on a sunny day. Have you seen my son or not?"

"No, I, I didn't mean any disrespect, sir." He stuttered. "But before you came up here, before, before you..."

"Nigga, just say it!"

"I thought he was dead. At least that's what I heard."

"Dead? My son ain't dead. He just staying away because he did something, he thinks is not forgivable. But I have to talk to him so we can make this right."

"Sir, I, wish that was true. But I don't know about that."

Mason moved closer. "Even if I were to entertain this dead shit, are you saying you involved?"

His eyes widened. "Me, of course not!"

"Well who told you that?"

"I'm staying out of it." He jumped in his car and pulled off.

An hour later Mason was riding with Dasher inside of his truck. She just got her hair blown out, Dominican style, and it flowed down her back every time she turned her head. Instead of appreciating the beauty, his mind was on what he heard about Howard being dead, and he felt bad for not focusing solely on her.

Since they started spending more time together, he found out she was more than a pretty face. She went to church every week. Volunteered her time at the hospital holding abandoned babies. Donated her time and money between friends and family. At the end of the day, she was genuinely a nice person. The perfect addition for the good man he was trying to become.

Trying to become.

Trying.

"You hungry?" He asked.

"Are you okay?" She responded rubbing his leg.

He smiled. It was so like her to be concerned about his well-being. "I'm good."

"Because you seem distant. I understand if you are. I think we put too much into talking." He paused. "Sometimes it's best to remain silent. Either way I just wanted you to know I'm here."

He nodded. "I know you are. So, what you want to eat, Blakeslee?" He shook his head briskly. "I mean, Dasher."

She giggled. "It's okay."

Her easy-going attitude, for some reason in that moment rubbed him raw. "No, it's not okay. That's not your name. You deserve to be called by your name."

She looked down. "Yeah, you're right." She looked away. "I'm stupid."

He placed his hand on her thigh. "Look at me."

She looked at the window.

"Dasher."

She looked at him.

"I don't want you to be sorry either. I just want you to know that sometimes it's okay to stick up for yourself."

"I know." She nodded. "You're right. So, don't call me Blakeslee anymore. Or me and you gonna fight."

They both laughed and settled into silence.

"I'm happy I met you." She continued. "For some reason, I feel like, I feel like I need you. Like my life is going to be better with you in the picture."

He rubbed her thigh a bit more. "I'm dangerous."

"Then fuck up my life."

"No doubt."

Spacey was helping Minnesota put up a new vanity in her bedroom which included locked drawers. She could have hired someone else to do the job, but she was being frugal with her money. Nobody knew what she was preparing to buy but whatever it was, it was big.

"This should hold you over for sure." Spacey said after screwing in the last nail for the drawer. He opened and closed it. "Works well enough."

She walked up to it and rubbed her hand over the expensive paneling. "Thank you."

He sat the screwdriver on the vanity. "Can I ask you a favor?"

She sat on the edge of her bed. "What's up?"

"As you know my fiancé doesn't have a lot of friends. That's one of the reasons I like her to be honest. Not easily swayed. So, I want her embraced into the Wales family. I want her to know since she married me, it'll all be good."

"What that got to do with me?"

He walked up to her. "I'm just saying, if you could spend a little time with her...maybe throw her a bachelorette party that would be nice."

"I'm not gonna be able to do that shit." She laughed.

He frowned. "Why not? You my sister and I'm—."

"For starters I'm not about to have no party for no fat bitch whose wedding is on the same day my birthday party was supposed to be."

"Are you serious?"

"Do it look like I'm playing?"

"It don't look like you playing but I can't believe you're this fucking selfish!"

"Spacey, say something to me that you haven't already. But understand this, I'm sick of everybody calling me selfish for speaking my mind. Granted, I had a lot of shit with me. And I didn't make the right decisions all the time. But I was a kid growing up around coke money. If you ask me, I should be allowed a learning curve or two. But I ain't there yet.

So, in the meantime, I don't have no time for no fat bitch or my fake ass brother. Thanks for putting together my dresser, bitch."

She got up and walked out the door.

CHAPTER EIGHTEEN

Holding her LV bag, Minnesota strolled up to a house she hadn't been to in years. So much had happened, and she allowed time to separate her from someone she cared about greatly. But she could no longer let things go as they were.

Taking a deep breath, finally she knocked. When nasty Natty appeared, she folded her arms across her chest. "What do you want, Minnie?"

She smiled. "No hello? I mean, how you been?"

"What you want?"

She shrugged. "I was kinda hoping to stop by and see what you've been doing. Play catch up. Maybe go get our nails done or something. Yours look like they could use a manicure." She giggled.

Silence.

Minnesota cleared her throat. It was too soon to joke. "So, what's up?"

"I haven't heard from you since I was shot by your people. What you thought, just because your father gave us some money things would be okay?"

"*Some* money? As I recall he gave you a million dollars."

"Yeah he did. And I saw a few thousand dollars. But my mother ran off with the rest." She shook her head. “But you were my friend. And I would have never done you like you did me. That shit hurt.”

Suddenly Minnesota felt stupid for stopping by. A call would have been better than a pop up. But she was hoping that if Natty saw her face, that she would feel it was impossible to close the door on their friendship. And now she felt all was in vain.

“You’re right. It was nice to see you anyway.” Minnesota turned around to leave.

“Bitch, did I tell you, you could go? Get the fuck over here.”

Minnesota smiled, turned around and walked into the house.

An hour later the girls were mostly caught up on life.

They talked about the death of Harris. The death of Arlyndo, Bet and so much more. They even addressed Banks being born a woman. But in that arena Natty wasn’t clueless. Nasty was briefed a lot about Banks on the streets already. Still, Minnesota fine-tuned the details.

"So how have you been?" Minnesota took a deep breath. "I been talking non-stop and I haven't heard anything from you."

"I'm better these days. But after I was shot, it was tough work getting back to who I was. Because I limp a little. I think it will be for life." She looked away and then looked down. "I guess, the thing that hurt the worse...I mean...why didn't you come see me? I don't get it."

"If I told you, you probably wouldn't believe me."

"Try me."

"After you were shot my father had me kidnapped. He was beefing with Mason and, I don't know, I guess he was going to take us to this island to get away from everything. But I didn't want to leave Arlyndo, so we ran away. And then Mason tried to kill me while I was with them to get revenge on my father. I basically ended up in a ditch and Arlyndo found me. Had he not, I would've been dead."

"Whoa. Sounds like a lot."

"After a while we had no choice but to link back up with his and my family and then eventually back here. So much happened, Natty, so much that I didn't get a rest at all until this year."

"Wow, I don't know what I expected but it wasn't that."

"I wouldn't lie about it either. I wasn't posted up at home living my best life. I was in a living nightmare. Still am now." She looked down and fiddled with her fingers.

"Such a nightmare where you couldn't call?"

"No. You deserved so much better than that, Natty." She placed her hand over her heart. "And I am sorry because you are a good friend."

"Stop." Natty was on the verge of a hard cry. "I, I get it now."

"I really missed you. To be honest I think you're the only person who would have truly understood what was happening. My father is a mess."

"Your father or your mother?"

Minnesota laughed. "Okay let's be clear, despite how my father was born I still consider him to be my father." She wiped her tears away.

"Me too, girl. I just didn't know what the criteria was since all this new information came out." She threw her hands up. "That shit still fucking me up to this day. Banks fine ass is a woman? Nah!"

"I get it. But it's the same for us. I had a mother who died and now I have a father who doesn't respect or love me. I think he wants me gone."

"I doubt that."

"Again, I wouldn't lie. I forgave him for forgiving Mason. I understood that in war things happen. But

I can't forgive him for thinking that I don't need guidance because I'm a little older. Or for thinking I don't need a father more than ever."

"Maybe Banks is dealing with a lot himself."

"He should, since he had two babies by Mason's wife."

"What?" She yelled. "You fucking lying!"

"I'm not! It's gross!"

"Rich people can do anything." She paused. "So, what about us, Minnesota? You had to come over here for something."

"I just want you back in my life, Natty. Is that okay with you?"

After leaving Natty's house, Minnesota popped up over Myrio's. She knew she shouldn't have gone but she missed him. And since their last conversation didn't end so well, she was hoping to remedy the situation.

It took a few seconds, but he finally opened the door and stood in the way. "What you doing here?"

"Are you gonna let me in?" She was hoping that since she had success with Natty that the same would've happened with him. "Please."

"I don't have time for games these days."

"It's not a game. We had a disagreement. Nothing more or less. It doesn't mean that I don't wanna see you. Or deal with you anymore."

"But I'm not sure I want the same. I mean, shit got strange between us. Too strange for my taste."

"Myrio, please don't do this." She stepped closer. "I'm begging you."

"It's not about please it's about respect. And you gonna have to give me more if you want me in your life."

"I'm trying to fix things now. That's why I'm here. Can you let me in to talk?"

"I'm not sure about all that because you spoiled. I don't care about you being rich. That's your father's money anyway. What I care about is dealing with a grown ass woman who can handle me."

"So, you're saying it's over?"

"I'm saying turn around and get the fuck back in your car. Period." He slammed the door in her face.

After dismissing Minnesota abruptly, Myrio locked the door and walked deeper into his house. Strutting into his bedroom he grabbed his cell and flopped on the edge of the bed. When he made a call he said, "Yeah, she popped up like you said. The shit was wild."

"Good." A male responded. "Did you play her from a distance?"

"Yep." He grinned. "I fucked up her head too. Saw it all over her face."

"Rich bitches think everybody gonna bow down to them. It's best she learns now."

"You not lying."

"Okay I'll let you know what's the next step later. But don't keep her waiting too long. From what I hear she has a short attention span."

"I'm on it. You can count on that."

CHAPTER NINETEEN

Shay was in the pool within the Louisville mansion with Derrick, straight fucking. They were both naked from the waist down and as she sat on his lap his dick was nestled firmly inside her body.

Every time she rose, he pulled her back down and she squeezed the inner walls of her vagina like she was ringing out a wet rag. He never experienced sex so sensual in his life. They may have had their problems but when it came to fucking it was as if they were business partners.

No detail went overlooked.

After they were done, she kissed his lips softly. "You gonna tell me what's on your mind now? Because I put it down on you and you still acting a bitch. I—"

"You really don't wanna know."

"For once can you answer my question without it being such a big deal?"

"Okay, I'ma ask you straight up. Were you going through my phone again?"

She got up and sat next to him in the water. "Yeah. I go through it all the time. You just finding that shit out?"

It wasn't funny. "I like how you don't think that's a problem."

"Derrick, I made clear that since we're together you will be open to inspection at any given time." She threw her hand up, splashing water in the process. "If you weren't such a whore, I would trust you more."

"Fuck is you saying? We live together. You think I would allow that if I didn't want this relationship?"

"Well, you've been talking on the phone a lot in private. If you're not cheating what is it about? Tell me that."

"I don't want to get into all of that right now."

"Derrick, I'm about to fight you hard. Punches, scratches and the works." She stood in front of him, ready for the battle. "And I know you a man and you're going to beat my ass when I'm done, but I'm tired of playing games with you. Now what's been going on?"

"I been asking around about Tobias. Because, I mean, you don't think pops gay, do you?"

"What? Of course not! Why would you even say that?" She laughed.

"Well, what does he see in Tobias?"

"I don't know." She shrugged up and down repeatedly. "Whenever they're together they're laughing about this and that, like two bitches. Seems soft to me. But I don't get gay. Maybe he looks at him like a son. I mean—."

"Derrick." Mason entered the pool house holding a glass of wine. The man never drank wine. They both looked at each other.

"Just wanted to let you know that Tobias moved in. He's staying in Arlyndo's room."

Derrick stood up. "Why he moving in here? He got enough money to get his own place."

"I don't gotta answer that question. This my house."

Derrick saw black. "Pops, what is your thing with this dude?"

"He's like a son to me."

"*Like a son?* But you got sons already. Oh, so now that Patterson and Arlyndo dead you adopt a grown ass man? Forgetting all about me?"

"Don't be stupid. We made a connection since we're doing business. I'm not going to see him out on the streets. Don't worry, it won't be forever. For now, he's staying here. I just thought you should know."

When he walked out Derrick did his best to remain calm, but he was literally trembling. It was one thing for him to spend a lot of time with Tobias but a whole 'nother thing to have him move into their home.

"I think we should go see my father." Shay said.

He got out of the pool and snatched a towel off the rack, causing the rest to topple to the floor. "Fuck I wanna see that nigga for?"

"If he put him out there has to be a reason. Maybe we should find out what it is."

Banks was in the gym when suddenly another migraine knocked him off the treadmill. Instead of getting up right away he laid on the floor and looked up into the ceiling. He didn't know where the pain originated but it was definitely taking over most of his life.

When it subsided a little, he grabbed a towel off the rack and wiped his sweaty face. Taking a deep breath, he stood up and walked to the bathroom. But his vision was blurred and made it hard to see.

Once inside, he moved the prescriptions around in the medicine cabinet, which mostly consisted of his hormone medication. After a deep search, he finally found some powerful medication. Only a few were left.

The dosage said one pill.

He removed two.

Jersey walked into the bathroom. "Honey, Shay and Derrick are here to see you. They look upset."

He frowned and turned on the sink. "For what?" He placed water into the palm of his hand and popped the pills.

"I don't know." She walked closer. "They said they need to talk to you though. Are you okay? Still in pain."

"I'm fine. Let me go see what's up." He walked out and she turned off the sink.

Five minutes later he strutted into the living room where they waited. Their visit was confusing because Derrick and Banks hadn't seen eye-to-eye for a while. Especially after he cut the man's toe and the disrespect recently at dinner.

"Are you okay, Shay?" He thought she may have been pregnant.

"I'm fine."

He nodded. "Okay, well what do you want?" He looked at both of them seriously.

"Did something go on with you and Tobias?" She asked.

Banks shuffled a little and crossed his arms over his chest. "Why?"

"Because he lives with us now."

Banks glared.

The moment she saw his expression, she knew there was more to the story. But getting it out of Banks would be easier said than done.

Walking around them, he flopped on the sofa. "What is Mason's thing with this dude?" He said mainly to himself. "Why won't he let him go away?"

Shay smiled.

Her father didn't like him either.

They sat on the sofa too. "I don't know." Derrick said. "But I think we should start working together to find out what's really up. That is if you're up to it."

"What makes you think I need your help?" He glared. "Whatever I decide to do, if anything, can be done easier if I go at it alone."

"Because he lives with us now, dad. I know you don't wanna hear this, but maybe we should stick together. At least this one time."

Spacey was in the kitchen making spaghetti for himself and his fiancé when his father called. There was soft music playing in the background which meant Banks was in a sad mood. Not only that, he didn't talk to him often during the week, so he immediately expected something was wrong.

Turning the eye down on the stove, he quickly answered. "Hey, pops! Everything okay?"

"You ain't been home lately. You good?"

He cleared his throat. "Yeah, just wanted to spend more time here."

"Understood. Your fiancé' still has that job at the hospital, right?"

He frowned. "Yeah, for now. Why?"

"Does she have access to Jovian? I remember her saying something to me about it after dinner. Didn't need it then. But I need it now."

He walked out of the kitchen. "Yeah, I think she has some in the cabinet. Why, what's up?"

"The headaches are bothering me more. It's fucking up my mind and I have a lot to work out."

Spacey sighed because if there was one thing about his father, it was that he hated doctors. "I know you despise hospitals and everything, pops, but you really need to see a doctor. With the way things have been happening in our family, I can't lose you too. Not after ma."

"Why would you even say something like that?"

"I'm not wishing anything on you. You know that. I just, I mean, I just think you should take better care of yourself that's all. Shay moving on with her life and Minnesota will be eighteen in a few. You need to be there for the twins. And for whatever you got going on with Jersey."

"The divorce is finalized. She'll be my wife soon."

"Even more reason for you to do better." He shrugged. "Please, pops go get help."

"Get me the pills and I'll come by later to scoop them up."

"Okay, pops. I love you."

"Love you too."

Spacey ended the call and took a deep breath.

Walking into the bedroom he opened the medicine cabinet. He didn't see the Jovian inside. Still, he recalled seeing them somewhere.

So, where were they?

Going through his wife's drawers and pushing her panties and bras aside, he finally found a bottle of pills.

But they weren't Jovian's.

Instead, they were weight loss medication.

To say he was heated was an understatement. After all, he made himself clear on how he liked his women and it was obvious she wasn't getting the picture. He knew what would happen if he continued to allow the disrespect. So, he had to remedy the situation A.S.A.P.

One hour later when she got home, he was sitting on the couch, waiting for her in the living room like a mad man. Nothing about his facial expression was positive and she felt it immediately.

"How was your day, sweetheart?" She asked placing her Gucci purse on the couch before giving him a kiss on the lips. His lips were so stiff her mouth bounced back.

"Not too good." He clasped his hands in front of him.

She frowned and tried to prevent from farting. "Is everything okay with Banks?"

"Get on the scale."

She laughed. "What?"

"Get on the fucking scale." He pushed it toward her with his big toe. It wasn't until that time that she saw it was there.

"Spacey, what is this? I mean, I don't understand."

He rose and cracked his knuckles. I wasn't raised to beat on women. But if you make me say it again, I may lose reason and drop your big ass. Now get on the fucking scale." He pointed at it again.

Kicking off her shoes quickly she jumped on the scale. She was ten pounds lighter than his preference. "I thought I told you I didn't want you changing anything."

"I know, but, but there was this dress. And I loved it so much. But they couldn't take it out anymore so I could fit it. And I wanted to look good for –"

He walked toward the door. "Get the fuck out."

"Spacey, you promised not to do this again!"

"Get out of my house! Now!"

"But it's mine!"

"Nah. My name on the deed and I bought it for you!"

Tears began to stream down her face immediately. "Spacey, I don't have anywhere to go. My parents disowned me the moment they found out I was going to marry into the Wales family. And my friends, well, you're all I got."

"You should have thought about that before you disrespected me. Now if I tell you again, I'ma lay hands on you. Bounce! Now!"

Banks had grabbed the pills from Spacey and was on his way to the doctor's office. The pain he was feeling these days made him believe something was seriously wrong. And there was so much to live for despite him feeling alone in the moment.

When he made it to the doctor's office, he was forced to fill out a form. He hadn't been to a doctor in years and dreaded the process because of his transition. Just sitting in the waiting room gave him anxiety.

Would he sign up as a man or woman?

This was important due to the level of care needed. And because he didn't know what was wrong.

After five minutes of waiting, he was in the doctor's office. The moment the door opened; he was surprised to see a male doctor. He didn't know who Q. Lipman was, but the condescending stare put him on pause.

Rude as fuck, Dr. Quincy Lipman flipped over his application with great attitude. "Your chart says you're female." He released the final page as if it were dirty.

Banks cleared his throat, but his voice was still too high. "Yes. I mean, not anymore."

"*Not anymore*?" The doctor glared. "What exactly do you want from me again? Because I don't operate in those types of fields. Or those types of people."

"I'm not here about my transition." He cleared his throat. "I wanted to get some help regarding the headaches I've been experiencing. And you're the best specialist. So I—"

"What is up with you people?"

"Excuse me?"

"You come in here with your issues and expect the world to clear them up. As if we're all playing dress up in your big playhouse!"

"Maybe I didn't make myself clear, all I want is some help with the headaches I been having. I don't want anything else from you."

"So, being a woman wasn't good enough? You had to make a feeble attempt at becoming a male?"

Banks wanted to kill him. "That's none of your business!"

"I disagree. It became my business the moment you entered my office."

"Let me get this straight, are you saying that you won't help me? Because I was born female?"

"On the contrary. I am *helping* you by reminding you of what you were born to be. A woman. Why would you mess up God's work? Nobody else may tell you this but I'm here to let you know. If you don't—"

"Say no more." Banks walked toward him violating his space. "But you're going to regret doing this to me." He glared.

"I doubt that very seriously."

"Trust me, it's a fact. You're the kind of man that walks around talking to people any kind of way. Well, today you made a big mistake. Huge."

"Are you threatening me?"

"No, now *I'm helping you*, by reminding you of this…there will come a day when everything as you know it will change. You won't see it coming. I'm strategic with my moves. But when it finally happens, it will be permanent. And this day will be the reason."

"Get out of this office!"

Banks laughed. "And if I don't exactly what are you going to do?"

"I'm not going to tell you again!"

Banks walk slowly out of the office but made mental notes on every aspect of the doctor's face. The sad part is this, in one minute, the doctor embodied every fear Banks had with the world.

And for that when the time was right, he would pay dearly.

CHAPTER TWENTY

Banks walked into the rehabilitation house he set up for Joey with the twins in tow. Since Joey was making progress, Banks ordered that the house be decked out with furniture, including his room to make him more comfortable. But under no circumstance was he allowed to leave.

And security was in place to carry out his wishes.

When the bedroom door opened, the moment Joey saw his father and his little brothers he jumped up excitedly. Playing with their little hands and feet, he was amazed at how much bigger and healthier they were. Even to the point of taking on Banks' and Mason's features.

"Wow, you came!" Joey said to Banks, while still playing with his brothers. He hugged him and then refocused on Ace, who was laughing happily, loving the attention.

Walid just stared, as if he was saying, *why are you touching us nigga*?

"I had to check on you. To make sure you're good." He paused. "So, how are you?"

"I'm doing okay. Could be doing better if I was home."

Bank sat the twins inside their carriers on the rug. Joey immediately dropped to his knees and began to play with the boys.

"Is everything okay here? You're eating? Getting the two hours of fresh air in the backyard?"

"Pretty much." He looked back at him. "I just wanna go home."

"Not now. It's too soon."

Joey looked down. "Well, why not? I haven't touched drugs in months."

"You shouldn't have touched them at all. I'm still not understanding how you went this route in life."

Joey sighed deeply. "I don't know, pops. Kinda mad people keep asking me the same thing over and over." He rose and sat on the bed. "I just, I just wish you weren't so judgmental."

"It's not about being judgmental! You know what that shit we pump does to people. And you decide to do it anyway? You better than that shit."

"And still you sell it." He threw his hands up. "If I'm guilty, you are too."

Banks glared. "Be careful, son. I sell drugs because I wanted a future for my family. Not because I don't care about those who take it. At the end of the day niggas are going to get product from somewhere. Might as well get quality shit from us."

"Says every drug dealer everywhere."

"Be easy. I'm still your father."

Joey looked down. "I'm sorry."

Banks didn't come there to battle. "Anyway, I'm here to see how you're doing. If you want me gone that's fine too. But you won't leave here until I feel it's the right time."

"No, I'm, I'm glad you came. Please don't go. Outside of the nurse you have checking on me, I'm tired of seeing these dudes faces around here."

Banks laughed. "I made the workers all men because I didn't want you having any distractions. Your sobriety is serious to me."

"If that's the case you did a good job."

Banks nodded and suddenly his headache rocked.

Again.

Banks immediately sat on the edge of the bed and when Joey saw his father's pained expression, he rushed over to him. "Dad, you good?"

He rubbed his temples. "I'm fine. I have to leave though."

"You sure you're fine?"

"Yeah." He picked up the twins. "I'll get up with you later."

Later on, that day, Banks met with Preach at their favorite bar. Earlier in the evening Preach said he had to discuss something important, so Banks made the meeting priority.

And after having a few beers, Preach got down to the heart of the matter. "I'm not positive, but I think somebody is making a move on you soon."

Banks laughed. "What you talking about? Everybody getting money on the streets because of our coke. So where is the problem?"

Preach looked around and back at Banks. "That was loud, sir. I normally know you to be more discreet. Any louder and the police would have heard us."

Banks shook his head. "Sorry, man. This headache has been driving me crazy. Making it hard for me to think straight."

He frowned. "I didn't know you were still experiencing migraines. I'm sorry."

"It's cool. It has to be."

Preach sighed deeply. "Well this won't make it any better. But like I said, I don't know who, but someone is actively trying to take you down. The person may be on the inside."

"Who told you that?"

"One of our men who felt comfortable coming to me since I'm first in command."

"So, he didn't tell you anything else?"

"It was all basic. Some girl the informant was dealing with, a white girl I believe, said she had it on good authority that the people around you would fall. She didn't say how."

Banks leaned back. "Well that's not going to be enough. I need you to find her ASAP."

"Already on it."

"Well what's the plan? Because, I can't have my kids fucked with. You know that."

"Let's just say the same person who told me is posted up in a location only I know about."

"I need to know too, Preach. The moment you do."

"Trust me on this, boss. I'll find out. I don't want to involve you yet. It's not necessary. I'm trying to be easy now but eventually she will have to tell me everything or she'll die."

"I have two young babies and—."

"I have your family in mind every day." Preach said with a hand over his heart. "She'll talk to me. Or she'll be done."

“Thanks, because with everything I got going on, treason is the last thing I need right now.”

He nodded in agreement. “How are your young sons?”

“They’re growing. Eating. Ace is happy but Walid is a little mean. He’ll grow out of it.”

“Let’s hope so, sir.” Preach grabbed his drink and took a large sip. “I have a little boy who’s gotten meaner since the day he was born. Thought he would grow out the shit too. Never happened. Just got worse.”

Banks laughed. “Don’t wish that shit on me. I already have snakes in my camp.”

“Don’t we all.”

CHAPTER TWENTY-ONE

The moment Jersey walked into the new place Banks liked to clear his mind, the nursery, Banks knew it would be a problem. Being with the boys unconsciously reminded him of better times, when Mason and he were kids. Except he didn't know he was living vicariously through them.

"Hey, honey. I was looking all over for you."

"Wanted to spend some time with the boys before Gina put them to sleep." He sighed. "Have you noticed how mean Walid has gotten?"

"He's just a baby, he'll grow out of it."

"Let's hope so." Although she gave him a dry response, he also noticed how Walid seemed to take pleasure at slapping his brother's head when they were in the crib together. As if asserting dominance. "Something is off."

"Yeah, maybe you're right."

She sighed. "So, where have you been?"

Banks shook his head. In the moment, she reminded him of Bet. Hawking. Pressing. Watching. "Why do you act like you haven't seen me in years?"

"Do you really want me to answer that?"

"Jersey, we sleep together every night."

"I hear you and maybe it's me, but I get the impression that when we were sneaking around that worked for you more. And now that you have me at your disposal it seems all you want me to do is—."

"Jersey, my head is rocking. We can talk later but give me a little peace."

"I give you peace when you sleep at night. Right now, I want you to look at me how you used to."

"If I wasn't in pain, I would be able to."

"Banks, I need you!"

"Not everything is about you. Some things go deeper."

"When will we spend more time together again? Can you at least tell me that?"

"I'm working on..."

Suddenly, Banks' phone rang. Thinking it was Preach with more intel, he quickly grabbed it out of his pocket. When he saw it was from Mason he jumped up and smiled. "Hey, what you up to?"

"You feel like talking? Maybe grabbing a drink with me?" Mason asked.

Banks grinned. "Give me the details and I'm on my way."

Per usual, Banks and Mason were at the bar laughing about an incident that occurred when they were teenagers. This time the memory was about a girl who showed everybody her coochie in the bathroom at school. But when she pulled down her panties and it smelled like fish; she was labeled Sardine instead of Sardisha throughout high school.

Taking a sip of his beer, Banks said, "You always remember the craziest shit. Because on mothers, I forgot all about that."

"I don't know why but you're so fucking right." Mason said shaking his head while laughing. "My memory is long and spooky as fuck."

"She was a cute thing too. Which is why it fucked me up she smelled so bad." Suddenly, Banks' headache rocked harder. But he didn't want to let on for fear Mason would call off the night.

"But, Banks, I called you out here because I want to talk to you about something. Something important."

Banks readjusted in his chair. "I'm listening."

"I'm out the game."

The world rocked.

There were many things Banks assumed he would witness before he ever thought he would hear those words. He thought he would hear that the earth had stopped rotating. That the sun had fallen out the sky and that the moon followed closely thereafter.

But he never, *ever*, thought he would hear the words that Mason Louisville was out of the coke business.

"Why, man? The only reason I'm still in this shit is because of you!"

"Banks, I lost two sons. Two. And I'm looking for Howard as we speak. Right now, I'm in a position to rectify a lot of wrongs. And moving cocaine ain't in my heart no more."

"But you promised you'd never do this shit!"

"I know and I'm sorry."

"Well that ain't good enough." He pushed his drink out of the way. "Don't you remember the day I tried to get out the business? When I went to my island? Or the time I was gonna put white boy Trey on? I told you then that Bolero would never let me out and that Trey was my plan for the future. And you said not to do it. And that you had my back."

"Banks, don't—."

"Nah, you gonna listen to this shit." He pointed at him. "Because you said you would never leave me because I knew if you did, all of this shit would be on my head." He pointed into the bar with a stiff finger.

"I know, man. And I really am sorry. But what would have happened if I was committed to that mental institution? Even then you would've had to carry this shit alone. What's wrong with now?"

Banks shook his head. "So, what the fuck am I supposed to do now?"

"I'm going to put you on with my guys. They still hungry and ready to work."

"I don't wanna be put on with your guys. I want you to help like you promised."

"And I'm saying I can't, man. If I thought I could I would. But I really am done with all this shit. I got a girl. My sons. And a life."

"A girl huh?" Banks said through clenched teeth.

"Yeah. And the worst thing I can do for you is stay in the mix when it's not in me no more. Don't worry, I'm not dropping you today. I'm phasing out in two months."

"Who put you up to this shit?" Banks glared. "Huh?"

"Come on, Banks. I'm a grown man. You know that."

"Was it Tobias? Because if it is, I'm really starting to feel like I don't trust him with your well-being."

"He's a good guy."

"Did this nigga just say a *good guy*?" He looked around. "Are you serious? You haven't called anybody a good guy ever. Are you sucking this nigga's dick or something?"

"Hold up, what you just say to me?"

"I ain't got to repeat it because your eyes tell me you heard exactly what the fuck I said! You promised you would never do this shit and you broke a vow." He put his hand over his heart. "To me. And it means you not a man of your word. And I got no use for a person like that."

"I broke a vow? You fucking my wife!"

"Fuck that bitch!"

"Wow!" Mason said.

"You destroying me with this shit." Banks continued.

"I'm sorry you feel that way, brother. I would have hoped you would want to see me happy. I guess I was wrong."

"I will never let you get away with this shit, Mason. I hope you know this."

"Are you threatening me?"

"Have you ever known me to say shit I don't mean?"

CHAPTER TWENTY-TWO

Spacey was asleep in his bed when his phone rang. It wasn't like it was the first call he received. His fiancé hit him a total of 172 times and he loved every minute of it. She didn't burn down his line just because she was in love, although that much was certain.

At the end of the day she called him like a maniac because she didn't have anywhere to go. No friends. No family.

No future.

And so, Spacey owned her.

After taking his sweet time crawling out of bed, and sliding on his silk pink robe, slowly he opened the front door where she was standing in the rain. Her makeup had run down her face and she unfortunately lost too much weight, which irritated him even more.

"Spacey, please don't do this." She wept. "I'm sorry. I should have never disrespected your wishes."

"And yet you did anyway."

"I know, but if you give me another chance, I will make it up to you." She softly grabbed his hand. "Please, baby, can I come in?" She trembled. "I'm begging you."

Instead of answering, Spacey left the door open as he walked toward the kitchen like a bitter wife.

Slowly she entered, closing the door behind herself. As she stood in the middle of the living room floor, he prepared frozen waffles, eggs, bacon, potatoes, and homemade lemonade with lots of sugar and syrup.

When the meal was done, they both sat at the kitchen table as he slid over her plate. "Eat."

Luckily, since she hadn't eaten in days, she devoured the meal whole. The poor thing was famished because he even controlled her paychecks and their bank accounts.

Perhaps if she had a little money at her disposal, she may have been able to take care of herself by renting a room. But he saw how his father was able to control his mother and was eager to do her the same.

Plus, he received a little advice recently that served him well.

When she was done eating, she put her spoon down and took a deep breath. "Can I come home, Spacey?" She wiped her mouth and burped. "Please?"

He sat back. "How do I know I can trust you?"

"Because I'll never betray you again." She shook her head quickly from left to right. "I know we had an agreement and I know you like a certain thing."

"If you know all of this why would you try and change the program?"

"Because I was stupid. And thinking that if I was smaller, I'd look prettier in my dress for you. But I should've realized that you like me just the way I am. I get it now."

"We talked about this in great detail already. And you said you could remain the same. In fact, you said you were happy because you never met a man who wanted you the way that you were."

She sniffled. "It's true. It's just, all of the dresses I wanted to wear looked horrible for my frame. And I panicked."

"Then we'll have one made. What's the use of dealing with a rich man if you can't get what you need?" He sat back in his chair like, The Don, despite the pink robe.

She smiled, and wiped her tears, which smeared more black makeup down her face. "I promise, I will never disrespect you again. And I know you don't believe me but it's true."

"I believe you because you don't have a choice. If you fuck up again, you die. I'm powerful enough to get you killed. Do I make myself clear now?"

Banks had taken too many pain pills.

It made him loopy, but unfortunately there was work to be done. Besides, it was bachelor party night. To make sure the event went off without a hitch, he had it catered with dancers speckled throughout the ballroom.

Things were going smoothly, but unfortunately for Banks' attitude problem, Spacey wanted Mason and Tobias in the building too. Claiming he desired to keep the family together. But Banks believed he knew what their presence was really about. Tobias was Bolero's son and Mason was Bolero's friend, and Spacey always held secret aspirations for the kingpin lifestyle.

As Tobias and Mason laughed happily across the room, as if Banks wasn't even in the building, Banks felt his temples pumping.

In his mind, this time his pain had less to do with migraines and more to do with rage. After all, he put up with Mason's antics for years. The fact that someone could come in and change him so easily, caused him to be severely outraged.

Where was the justice?

Why wasn't Mason willing to change for him?

Seeing Banks' rage, Derrick walked over to him. "I see Spacey is enjoying himself."

When Banks looked at his son, he smiled at the big pretty girl giving him a lap dance. In fact, all of the females were large, thick and pretty, which the world knew was Spacey's preference.

"That's good," Banks said as he redirected his focus on Mason and Tobias. "It's his night."

"So why is my father and Tobias acting like it's about them? If you ask me, they as thick as old cheese."

Banks blinked a few times. The pills had him off. "Yeah, I see that shit too."

"Well have you thought about what we should do?"

"Mason mentioned something about some broad he dating." He looked at him. "You know where she rests her head?"

Derrick smiled. "Of course, I do."

"Give me the information." He focused back on Mason.

Derrick nodded. "But you know, if you kill her, it may bring him and Tobias closer together."

"I don't give a fuck no more. Your father stepping out of the business and fucking up my plans. Why should he move so easily with a new bitch too?"

"I agree. And I wanna help."

Banks looked at him. "Are you sure?"

"Haven't been surer about anything else in my life. Tell me what you want me to do and it's done."

CHAPTER TWENTY-THREE

The house was decorated outstandingly courtesy of Mr. Banks Wales.

To ensure the evening was perfect, he made sure every area was showered with the color scheme. Soft pink, cream and salt gray. He also spared no expense since this was the first of his children to get married.

This included heightened security.

As the soldiers who were speckled throughout the property stood on guard, they looked dapper wearing expensive tuxedos. So smooth, that they almost looked like members of the wedding party. But make no mistake, their purpose was to do one thing and one thing only.

Defend the Wales family with their very lives.

Banks was still holding court with the caterers when Minnesota approached him from behind. She looked beautiful in her soft pink dress, with her hair swept up in a bun. "Dad, can I talk to you for a moment?"

Banks wasn't in the mood, besides his head thumped.

Still, he nodded to the staff to walk away. When they were gone, he turned his attention to his daughter. "What is it, honey?"

"Everything looks nice."

He wasn't expecting a sweet response. But Minnesota had buttered him up before, only to strike as deadly as a venomous snake moments later. So he wasn't impressed.

"Yeah, Jersey did a good job of making sure all of the details were cared for. I just wrote the check."

"You always do."

He couldn't tell if she was being nice or sarcastic. But he reasoned it didn't matter anyway. "What do you need?"

"I wanted to tell you that I know I've been out of sorts lately. It's just that had you apologized for not throwing my party, I would have felt better."

"If I recall I did apologize. I also made it clear that this family needs this wedding."

"Why do you keep saying that?"

"I have my reasons."

"Give me one. Please."

"Well, mainly because after Harris and your mother died, we had a dark cloud over our heads. Until the twins were born. And I figured this wedding could provide a little light."

"The thing is, the dark cloud never left me. I'm still hurting by everything that happened to my brother, my mother and me. Still, I forgave you for forgiving Mason after he tried to have me killed. I realized that sometimes people act crazy during war. But it doesn't mean I gave you a license to abandon me. I still need you, daddy. Did you even notice I was gone? Or that I moved?"

"What are you talking about? I supported you more than I've ever done the boys. Ever since you were born. Without going into detail, you and I both know you share my direct bloodline. And Spacey, Harris and Joey knew that. And I was wrong for treating them differently for so many years."

"So, you sacrifice my happiness now?"

"Yes. If that's what you want to call it." He paused. "But don't worry, I bought you an excellent gift."

She glared. "Your money doesn't work on me anymore."

"I doubt that. But—."

Banks' speech was cut short when Jersey walked inside wearing a nightgown. But what Minnesota noticed caused her stomach to swirl.

"Hold up, is she pregnant? *Again*?"

Banks looked at Jersey as if he had almost forgotten. "Yeah, but I thought you knew."

"No, I didn't. I haven't been here, remember?" She glared at her belly with disdain. "Is Mason the father again?"

Banks frowned. "Don't be stupid. We went about things our way this time. And you should be happy. You have a baby sister on the way."

A little girl?

Minnesota was infuriated.

Her body trembled and her hands clutched in tight fists. She would have snatched that infant vagina out of her if she had longer hands. In her opinion it appeared that Banks wanted nothing more than to build another family to replace the ones murdered.

Sort of like a do over.

"No, you didn't tell me! You have Ace and Walid. Why do you go and add another girl?"

Jersey stepped up. "Me having this baby is not a slight to you. We want you to be a part of—."

"I'm not talking to you, bitch!" She said pointing at Jersey. "I'm talking to my father."

"Minnesota, this baby is coming whether you like it or not." Banks said firmly. "You're eighteen now. If you don't like it, you can get out. You been gone anyway. Now is there anything else?"

Silence.

"Is there?" Banks said louder.

"No, dad. Not now. But there will be later. You'll see."

Banks was securing Spacey's tie in the lounge within the mansion. In less than two hours he would be a married man. He was proud of him in a way that couldn't be explained but he did his best to express himself anyway. "How do you feel?" Banks asked.

"I'm nervous mostly."

Banks nodded. "We all get the jitters sometimes. As long as you're sure she's the right one, thing should go smoothly." He looked into his eyes. "She is the right one, right?"

"Yes." He shrugged.

"Well, at least you know that you made the right decision."

"I hope so because I want to be married to her for at least five years."

Banks frowned. "What you mean at least five years?"

"Well you don't expect me to keep the same wife forever, do you? What happens when she gets older? I don't want no old ass wife. I rather keep them young and soft."

"Son, you should not be looking at marriage that way."

"Why not? You getting a new wife. Why shouldn't I have one too?"

Banks was still staring at Spacey when Joey walked into the room, dressed dapper in a gray pinstripe suit.

Excited to see his brother, Spacey rushed up to him and pulled him into a one arm hug. "Joey, you here!"

Joey grinned. "Yeah, pops sent for me."

Spacey smiled at his father and Banks placed a heavy hand on his shoulder. "I'll leave you two alone."

When he left Spacey said, "You look good!" He examined his eyes. "Are you…I mean…"

"Yeah, man. I'm clean."

Spacey hugged him again. "How?"

Joey looked behind him to make sure Banks was gone. When he confirmed the coast was clear he took a deep breath. "Pops hired some people to do it guerilla style."

Spacey shook his head. "That sounds like him."

He moved closer. "It does but for real, I think, I mean, something's wrong with dad."

Minnesota was moping around the mansion, waiting for the wedding to be over until she took her seat in the large dining room where the ceremony would be held. The windows were open showcasing the massive backyard which was speckled with pink and gray flowers.

Everything was on color scheme.

Booooooooooooooooo. She thought.

People were walking around and preparing for the ceremony, as if she wasn't there and she was devastated and angry, until Myrio walked in and sat next to her. "Myrio?" She said as if he didn't know his name. "I, I didn't think you were still coming."

"Why, I'm your date right?"

"Yeah, but I thought after the fight and you closing the door in my face. I mean, you—"

"That was the past. This is now." He kissed her lips. "Cheer up. Love is in the air." He raised his arm showing the watch.

"You didn't have to wear that today."

"I did. You gave it to me."

She grinned brightly.

He pulled her toward him, and she rested her head on his chest. "Thank you for coming." A tear fell. "Thank you."

The ceremony was beautiful, short and sweet.

And in the end, Spacey was officially a married man. His wife, despite all she had been through, seemed overjoyed and relieved to be Mrs. Lila Wales.

Poor thing.

Some would say she signed her death certificate.

Some would be right.

Now, at the reception, which was also in the house, the music blared and everyone except a few seemed to be in the mood to celebrate. For instance, one of the Louisville men, Derrick, was sitting in the corner of the living room where the main ceremony was taking place with Shay propped on his lap like an old purse.

Every time he moved his leg to the beat of the music, Shay's titties bounced.

"Did Banks say what he had planned?" She asked. "For your father?"

"Yep, he's going after Dasher."

Shay smiled. "Good. She thinks she cute anyway." She paused. "You ready to step up? And prove yourself to my dad?"

"I couldn't be more ready."

She nodded and when Spacey and his new wife eased onto the dance floor she sighed. "When do you think we're going to make that move?"

"I knew you were gonna ask me that shit."

"How you figure?"

"Women always wanna get married after they see another broad get hitched."

Her head fell backwards. "Hold up, did you just disrespect me?"

"So, you call the truth disrespectful?"

"I don't want to marry just anybody. I want to marry you. You know I always felt like we were made for each other. I don't see why things should change now."

"So, you're telling me you prefer to be Shay Louisville instead of Shay Wales?"

"You answer me this, am I a villain or not?"

He smiled, loving her answer. "You always talk so much shit."

She laughed and kissed his lips. "No for real, I know we argue a lot and I know sometimes you want to throw me out your house but I'm happy to be your girl. I'm used to being in relationships where things go too smoothly. With you I feel alive."

"You had one nigga. Stop acting like you been around."

"Shut up, bitch." She laughed.

"You must like when I beat that ass." He said.

"Don't get fucked up out here!" She giggled harder. "I'm just telling you how I feel. I really am happy that we're together. Finally."

He looked into her eyes and could tell she was being honest. Had somebody told him she would be his main frame he would have laughed them out of the building. But she was mysterious, beautiful and ready for war. Those traits alone made him feel like they were a good match.

That's not to say she was without flaws.

Going through his phone and car was annoying, especially when she made conspiracy theories about him dealing with other females based off things like girl names on cashier receipts. But at the end of the day Derrick wasn't cheating because at the moment they were good and that was the bottom line.

"You cute or whatever." She laughed. "But you always talking—" Her sentence was cut when Mason walked over to the couple.

"Shay, let me talk to my son for a few minutes." She looked at Derrick and when he nodded, only then did she rise and walk away. "She's very disrespectful."

Derrick shrugged because he didn't see any problem. "What's up, pops?"

Mason took a seat next to him. Taking a deep breath, he said, "I owe you an apology."

Derrick's eyes widened. "An apology. For what?"

"You've been needing me a lot lately, and I haven't been there. It's not because I didn't want to. It's just that I've been trying to get my mind together."

"Why? Because of ma? Because I know she still loves you."

"No, son." He waved the air. "I've moved on from her."

He glared at Dasher and looked back at his father. "Then what's wrong then?"

"My main issues are about Howard. In my heart, I know I should have handled him differently and I failed. I should've listened a bit more. But I don't want to do that with you."

Derrick tried to pretend he didn't care, but it was hard because he missed his dad. "What are..." he cleared his throat. "What are you saying?"

"I'm saying I'm sorry. For ignoring you over the months. I should have known that you needed me more. Instead I was distant. But now that I'm freed up on time, I'm going to make it better. Things won't always be great, but they'll be different."

It took Derrick everything in his power not to cry. Mason wasn't an emotional type of dude, so the fact that he apologized spoke levels.

"You don't know how much I needed that. Thank you, pops." He tried to hold back a tear, but one drip, dropped anyway.

Mason grabbed him in a one-armed hug, followed by two arms. With one hand behind his head he said, "I see you holding back tears. Sometimes, son, it's okay to be vulnerable. I'm learning that too."

They hugged a bit longer and then separated.

Derrick took a deep breath and had to relish in the fact that Tobias did good things for his father's mood.

"What made you come over now?" Shay was in the corner of the room watching and he was sure he would have to explain every detail later.

"I say why put off tomorrow what I can do today."

It was simple and it fucked up his head. "Thank you." It was the only words he could muster.

"No need to thank me, son." Mason took a deep breath. "Well, let me go get something to sip on. Enjoy the night. I know I will."

The lighting was nice and dim as Myrio and Minnesota danced. The day started out painful but now she was so happy to be in his arms.

"So, how are you?" He asked as they moved slowly.

"Why do I get the impression you're fishing when you ask me questions?" She looked at him and then laid her head on his chest again.

He pulled her closer. No room between them. "Not sure why. But you're right about one thing. There is a deeper reason as to why I'm asking."

"Okay, I'm listening."

"Now that you're a woman, what do you really want out of life? Do you want to be dependent on your father forever? Do you want to need his money no matter what? Or do you finally want freedom?"

"Are you asking me to be your wife?"

He laughed. "Marriage is not for me. It will never be."

That hurt. "I'm glad I found out now."

"Again, I prefer to be honest. You should know that by now."

"If I know nothing else." She paused. "But you're right, I do need to be independent." She looked across the room at Banks who was zeroing in on Mason and Tobias like a whole creep. "My father has proven he's only for self. That he doesn't care about anything but his new kids and Mason."

"I thought you liked the twins."

"I do. But his wife is pregnant again. This time it's a little girl. It's like he's trying to replace me or something. It's like he's trying to replace all of us."

Myrio frowned. "How is it possible for him to have kids with her?"

"He's rich. He could have another one of you if he wanted."

He laughed. "You probably right."

"Anyway, I want my own money. I don't want to ask him for anything."

"Have you thought about how you want to go about your freedom?"

She looked up at him. "Again, you're fishing, aren't you?"

"Maybe." He shrugged.

"I don't have many ideas." She sighed deeper. "I know it involves cocaine though. It's been my whole life."

He smiled. "Well maybe it's time to make your mark on the world."

"What you mean?"

"The thing about women is this, they're smart, they think about things in advance. Men don't always move the same way."

"My father does."

"I don't have to tell you how that proves my point."

Minnesota nodded her head. "I guess you're right."

"So maybe you venture out on your own. Maybe you start your own dynasty." He looked into her eyes. "Maybe I help you."

"What's in it for you?"

"Let's just say I'll take a commission off whatever we make."

"A commission huh?"

He pulled her closer. "And there are a number of ways for us to handle the payout."

Spacey walked over to the young couple, destroying the moment. "You mind if I dance with my sister?"

Myrio shook his head and walked away.

Spacey pulled her a little close and held her hand. "I don't want to fight with you anymore."

"Yes, you do. That's what we do."

"No, I don't. As a matter of fact, I think there will come a time when we need each other."

"Even though I destroyed your wife's feelings by not throwing her a party?"

He looked back at Lila's pretty face and then refocused on his sister. "Yep, because I'll buy another wife soon." He winked. "Anyway, I got you something." He reached in his pocket and pulled out a small red box before handing it to her. "Happy birthday."

She started crying.

"You okay? Did I do something wrong?"

She shook her head. "No, it's just that you, you're the only person who remembered it was today." He opened the box and put the diamond necklace on her neck.

A server took the trash away.

"It's beautiful." She smiled rubbing her fingertips over the diamonds. "Thank you. He forgot. He actually forgot."

"You're lying." He frowned. "Dad had to say happy birthday."

She shook her head. "No, he didn't."

"Whoa, try not to blame him. He's been having these weird headaches. And you know it's been crazy with the wedding and—"

"No more excuses. He forgot my birthday. And to make matters worse I don't think he really cares. So, if that's how he wants to carry things that's how I will carry things too."

"Please don't get into an altercation with Pops. The reason I walked over here was because I want my family together."

"You have a family, with your new wife."

"She'll give me a few kids. True. But then I'll have no use for her anymore. Besides, women change. I won't be around for the worst part. It's yucky."

"She's pregnant?"

He nodded yes.

She was a bit jealous. "Looks like she's going to have a baby the same time as you'll have a new sister."

"I know." They continued to dance. "I think it's cool. Your eyes tell me something else is wrong. Outside of what we talked about are you really okay?"

"I'm far from okay."

Spacey look behind him at Myrio who was talking to a few women in the corner. "The real reason I walked over here is to tell you this...your guy Myrio...I don't trust him."

"Why?"

"I don't know. Something about him seems dishonest."

Minnesota pulled her hand away. "Well you have to get used to him because he's not going anywhere. But I am."

"What does that supposed to mean?"

She smiled and walked away.

Jersey was making herself a plate when Mason walked up behind her while looking at her belly. "Wow, ya'll did it again huh?"

Jersey looked over his shoulder for Banks but didn't see him around. "I thought you didn't want me talking to you." She whispered.

"I don't."

She frowned. "Then what do you want?"

"Don't worry, I didn't tell him how you sucked my dick at the apartment. I'm keeping that between us."

She trembled. "Please...please don't do that. I, I just wanted you to let me go."

"So now I raped you? That's what you saying?"

"I didn't say that."

"I know you didn't. You were doing it so good. Extra spit and shit." He shook his head. "You were sucking it so hard I had to pull you off of it. I can tell you loved it." He smiled brighter. "Let me ask you something, you happy with Banks?"

She rubbed her belly with her free hand while the other one held the plate. "I'm home when I'm with him. I prefer saying it that way."

He smiled. "Well, you look good. I hope he makes you smile since I made you cry." He kissed her on the cheek and joined his pretty young girlfriend at the table.

She dropped the plate on the floor and ran in the opposite direction crying.

Mason and Tobias sat at a table within the Wales estate with their girlfriends. Banks originally shut down the idea of Tobias coming to the wedding, but just like the bachelor party, Spacey was adamant that he wanted them both there.

While Tobias, Dasher and Alexis were talking, Gina smiled at Mason as she walked across the room. Suddenly she seemed very familiar.

I know her from somewhere. He thought.

"Mason, you heard me?" Dasher asked.

"Oh, uh, yeah, I understand what you saying. But no man should fear another man. I don't care who he is."

He normally didn't do *small-talk* but he was feeling different these days. Like he was a man about the world.

"I'm not saying you should be scared but you should be cautious around certain people." She replied.

"They're not going to hear you." Alexis, Tobias' date said. "These men are super masculine and incapable of showing feelings or fear."

"Negative." Tobias said adjusting the collar of his suit jacket. "I don't have a problem admitting when I'm emotional. At times."

"Really? Because every time I ask you a question about us you close down a little." Alexis responded.

"That's because I know you want to hear a certain thing. And I want to take my time before I commit. To make sure it's right."

"Men hate commitment." Dasher added.

"What is commitment really?" Mason asked taking a sip of his drink. "In your opinion?"

"Don't walk into that door, Dasher." Alexis said. "I feel a trap coming on."

"Let her talk." Tobias laughed.

"I think commitment is being with one person exclusively. And making sure you spend the time to prove you're vested."

"So, if we lived across state lines and I didn't see you, but spoke to you every day, that's not commitment?" Mason asked.

"If that's what you're into." Dasher replied crossing her legs. "Personally, I could never be with a man I can't see on the regular. Call me old-fashioned but I need to be held and touched."

"We all know what you want to be." Mason laughed nudging her leg playfully.

"I know you're talking about sex but that's only one portion of what I'm saying."

"But it's still an important part." Alexis pointed at her.

"True." Dasher giggled. "But I can be with a man and not have sex. If the bond is deeper."

"Now you're confusing me. Are you trying to say every time we together, you're good with us just talking?"

"Nope not saying that either. I'm saying that there are certain times that you get around someone, where the energy can't be described. Love can transfer across races. And even sexualities if it's real enough."

"Now you doing too much," Mason said. "'Cause I don't care what you say, I'm not fucking no 'nother nigga."

The table busted out in laughter.

But across the room one man didn't find shit funny.

That man was Banks Wales.

Banks walked over to Derrick who was getting another drink from the bar. "Enjoying yourself?" He asked.

"I don't know if you can enjoy yourself at a wedding but I'm good."

Banks chuckled. "Let me ask you something, you ready to do what we talked about? With Dasher?"

Derrick shuffled a little. "I mean...I...she..."

"What's up?" Banks asked looking into his eyes. "You pulling out on me just like your father?"

"I don't know about all that. I'm not really sure if this is for me anymore."

"If this is for you? Nigga, you brought this shit to me! To my house!"

"I know but pops seems different now."

"That's the fucking problem! He too soft! He just told the caterers he wanted tea!"

"But why does it have to be soft? Maybe we should give him a little space. He's nice now."

"Nice, nigga we gangstas!" Banks laughed. "What did he say to you?"

He shifted a little. "What did who say?"

"Your father. Because a few days ago you were all about business and now you singing a different tune."

"Let's just leave this alone." He shrugged.

"Yeah, you right. I'll let her breathe. But what happens next is on you."

Bolero's driver made a right into the Wales estate after clearing security. Along with Bolero, in the car were his unclaimed daughters, Cassandra and mentally ill Roxana. Originally Bolero declined Spacey's invitation, but suddenly changed his mind at the last minute.

The plan was to make an entrance.

"When we get inside, we'll say hello and leave." Bolero said as he dusted lint off his suit.

Cassandra wiped her hair behind her ear. "Is my brother here?"

"Yes."

"Why are we here again?" Roxana asked.

"I have my reasons," he said.

"Well I don't like them." Roxana said. "I don't like them at all."

"You'll fall in line or I have another place for you in mind. It won't be as cozy as the hotel you're staying in. And trust me you won't like it."

When the night grew later, Tobias was led to the backyard by Spacey who left shortly thereafter. He didn't know why Banks requested to speak to him, especially on his wedding day, but he was happy to oblige. With the exception of the flower speckled throughout the lawn, the backyard was empty.

As Banks stood before him the moonlight shined above his head. Instead of speaking he stared at him for what seemed like an eternity.

"Sir, you wanted to talk to me?"

"I don't trust you."

Tobias nodded. "You definitely made that clear although I wish you would give me a good reason why. Everything I've tried to do is out of respect for you, your family and your daughter. Even if that meant leaving her alone."

"Except you didn't go away did you? Why?"

Tobias frowned. “That’s weird, you never said you wanted me to go away. You said you wanted me to get out of your house. I did that.”

“I assumed putting you out my crib meant putting you out my life. And yet you get up with my man’s instead.”

Tobias took one step closer. “I’m sorry what is this about again? Because I’m really confused now.”

“It’s about you not being smart. It’s about you making a big mistake.”

“Sir, I can leave your house now if you want. Spacey invited me and I thought you wouldn’t mind. But I can go if—”

“No, you can’t leave. Should’ve done that before. You won’t get another chance now.”

At that moment two men walked up behind Tobias, both dressed in tuxedos. Without another word, one of them placed a chain around Tobias’ neck and lifted him off his feet until his neck cracked to the left.

When he was dead, his body flopped to the ground.

Having committed a heinous act, Banks pulled his phone out of his pocket and made a call. “Come out back. I got something I want you to see.”

As Banks stared down at Tobias with a grin on his face, across the property, Minnesota was watching the scene with Myrio in the bushes. They originally went to the back to smoke a little wood and saw a murder instead.

"Oh my, God." She said covering her lips. "He just killed Bolero's son."

Myrio smiled.

Four minutes later Mason came running outside. When he made it onto the patio, he was devastated to see Tobias lying dead amongst the flowers.

Banks looked at his men. "You can leave us alone."

"Are you sure?" One of them asked.

Banks nodded and they disappeared into the house.

Seeing his friend, Mason felt dizzy. Dropping to his knees he placed a finger on the vein of Tobias' neck for his pulse. He was certainly dead. "What did you, what did you do?"

"What it look like?" Banks said uncaringly.

"Are you crazy, nigga? You just...you just killed Tobias!"

"And? You know how many bodies you have under your belt? Do I gotta remind you of all the blood shed? Now all of a sudden you're concerned about one more?"

"What the fuck is going on with you?" He threw his hands up. "I'm not understanding your mental state right now! Do you get what this will bring to you and yours?"

"Fuck is that supposed to mean?" Banks stepped closer.

"Bolero will never stand for this!"

"See that's what I'm talking about!" Banks said pointing at his face as if he sniffed a lie. "Not even a couple months ago you could have cared less about the heat that would come your way over something like this. And now all of a sudden you concerned? Are you on drugs or something?"

Mason grinned. "No, nigga, are you?"

"Nah, but I should have put him out of his misery the day he got off that plane with Bolero." Banks paced like a mad man. "But I let it slide. Because I thought about the future. But you were right back in the day, why should I consider the future when nobody else does?"

"The night I asked you to decide on Jersey or the twins, this man was the one who changed my mind." He pointed at his body. "This man was the one who forced me to think about what I was doing. And this is how you treat him?"

"I don't give a fuck about that nigga!"

Mason's world was rocked.

With Tobias dead he was suddenly going back to his old ways of thinking. Because at the end of the day, it was easier to make the *right* decisions when you had the *right* company.

But now he felt violent. A sensation that missed him for months.

And suddenly everything clicked.

Mason looked up at Banks. "What do you want?"

"What, nigga?"

"You did this for a reason. So, I'm asking you straight up, what do you want? Because I'm tired of playing games with you. If you want something from me, you gotta make yourself clear right now."

Banks walked a few feet away and turned back around. "I don't know what you're talking about."

"Stop saying the same shit over and over!" Mason nodded rapidly. "You do know what I'm saying because its written all over your face."

"And what's that?"

"Envy."

Banks laughed. "I'm supposed to be jealous of what? This dead ass mothafucka?"

"Yes! Why else would you not want me to be easy going? And calm. Something you preached for years. You never liked when I went berserk in the past, but you want me to act out now."

"Whatever, nigga."

"This was all set up so you could push my buttons. To see how far I would go." He stepped closer. "So, I'm asking you straight up, do you want me or not? No more games! Is it gonna be me and you or what?"

"You sound stupid! If anything, I was protecting you from this traitor!"

"I don't believe you. You weren't able to deal with me saying fuck it. You weren't able to deal with me not needing you. Not being pressed to be your friend. You even got my ex-wife pregnant twice. Still I didn't give a fuck. But this, this you knew would hurt me. And you did it anyway."

Banks looked at him. "Whatever."

"Oh yeah, I see it all in your eyes. You got the girl and the money, Banks. What's left but me?"

Banks' temples began to throb even more. He didn't know if it was because of what he had done or Mason's words. Either way he was in a lot of pain. Pain so severe he almost fell down until Mason caught him and helped him into a lawn chair.

"What's up, man?" Mason asked concerned. "You good?"

"Nah, I think something is wrong. Don't take me to a hospital. Please."

Suddenly Preach came running outside followed by three men. The moment he saw Tobias' body amongst the flowers he instructed the other two to get rid of his flesh. No questions were asked only actions were taken.

"Banks, I found out who the snake is." Preach said.

"Not right now." Mason said as he was preparing to call 911. "Something's wrong with Banks."

"Hold fast. This is important."

Mason looked at him. "Make it quick."

"I think Gina, the nanny, is Banks' grandmother. Where are the twins?"

CHAPTER TWENTY-FOUR

MANY YEARS EARLIER

Gina Petit was on her knees on the grounds of her modest Victorian style home in Richmond, Virginia. Tending to her garden, she was startled when her youngest daughter ran outside, wearing shorts that cut too far between her legs and stank up the seat, per usual.

"Mama," she stood by her barefoot and trembling.

"What, girl? You know I don't like to be bothered when I'm—."

"Mama, shut up and listen!" She covered her mouth. "It's Angie."

Gina dropped her trowel, stood up and dusted the soil off her knees. "You know we don't talk about her in this house. Ever."

Huge tears strolled down Carmen's face. "Mama, I know but, mama, she's dead."

Gina's eyes widened as she backed up into the large oak tree. Suddenly the earth seemed off balance as she passed out.

Later on that day, Gina overdosed on every detail about her estranged daughter's story since they were separated. After some time, she learned that she was murdered in a horrible way. During the holiday season Angie had gone to the store only to be robbed and killed with her daughter Blakeslee watching in the car.

The news caused her major pain.

Gina never wanted to separate from her daughter, but she felt Angie made her decision long ago after being given an ultimatum.

Stick with the family or be cut off for life.

Angie chose the cut off. First, when she married Peteery Thompson, who was nothing more than a bootlegger who made money selling moonshine. This, days before Gina specifically forbade the union.

In Gina's mind Angie violated again after Peteery beat her repeatedly, only for her to run into the arms of Dennis, Banks' father.

Angie told the world her mother hated her attraction to black men. But Gina and Angie's relationship was strained not because Gina chose to date outside her race, which was uncommon in Virginia in the eighties, but because the men she chose were unworthy of her daughter's love and the wealthy lifestyle Angie was accustomed.

The Petit family, who originated from France, made quite a living making products for people battling hair loss due to cancer. And after developing an effective serum that enabled quick hair growth days after final radiation treatments, the Petit family became millionaires many times over.

But Angie didn't care about wealth.

She felt weighed down by her mother's rules and regulations, and so she rebelled, eventually falling into the foster care system within the DMV area. But there was something else wrong with her daughter. Angie was mentally ill and due to brain tumors, often suffered from headaches which caused not only severe pain but mood changes.

And so, Gina worried constantly about her child, but always from a far. After all, it was Angie who chose to walk away from the family dynasty and live in squalor.

In Gina's mind, it was above her at that point.

She turned away from Angie and poured all of her imposing attention toward her other children. There was the oldest, Hercules Petit, whose father was born in the small-town Herculaneum, Missouri. And Aaron Petit, followed by the youngest, and wildest daughter, Carmen Petit.

Things were okay and Gina moved on with her life, until Angie's murder.

Now she had to do something.

After learning about the violent crime, she poured her resources and power, into trying to find her only grandchild at that time, Blakeslee Wales.

But she was in for the shock of her life.

After Angie's death, for years she went about searching for Blakeslee to no avail. She had seen her face on the news and so her heart poured out. She was determined to find her granddaughter. But it was difficult, and years later, it appeared that Blakeslee had fallen off the face of the earth.

Until her oldest son came to her with information that rocked her world.

On one fine day, she learned that Blakeslee had transitioned from a woman to a man. When Gina got over the shock, Hercules provided her with his address.

She wanted to meet him, but she realized it had to be in disguise. The reason was simple, she had to feel him out, knowing her daughter always perceived her involvement as intrusive. She was certain she gave those same opinions to her only child. She needed the upper hand.

With the right disguise, she set out on her adventure.

The first time Gina met Banks she was shocked at how well he transitioned into a man. So much so, that she called Hercules to be sure he had gotten the information correct. The person before her couldn't be her granddaughter. This was a man. And then she saw his eyes, that resembled her daughter's so much she cried silently.

Their first introduction occurred when he purchased his plane after gaining his pilot's license. It was Gina, disguised as a salesperson, who showed him around his new aircraft. She knew what she was talking about as she pointed out the features. This wasn't an unfamiliar zone for her. After all, Banks earned the love of flying honestly. Her husband, his grandfather, was a professional pilot until the day he died.

When they began to talk, she liked him immediately and secretly vowed to be there when she needed him the most. Whether he knew about her or not. It was also painfully obvious that although he loved his deceased mother, he could care less for the family he believed tormented her due to falling for a man of another race.

The second time she met him was on the worst day of his life. He had just gotten the news that his son, Harris Wales had died in a botched prison escape. Disguised as a nurse, she walked him outside to his car while consoling him as Shay, also dazed by the news, followed closely behind. Their moment together was brief, but profound for Gina, connecting them even more. Although rarely caught slipping, Banks was so distraught, that he hadn't realized that he met her twice.

No worries. There would be a third time.

With a lot of research, Gina could tell immediately that her grandson lived a life of crime. And she was determined that she would maintain eyes on him at all times. She intended to be successful. Because the one thing better than dope money, was old money, and Gina had lots of it.

With her investigators working hard she learned about Banks and Jersey's budding love affair. So, she introduced herself to Jersey while on an initial fertility appointment. Disguised as a woman supporting her daughter who was having fertility treatments in the waiting area, the two bonded immediately. Especially when Gina said she was a nanny for over twenty years.

Thirty minutes later, after Gina had given her tips on rearing children, Jersey said, "Oh my God, if I get pregnant, you don't think it would be possible to steal you away from the family you work for now do you?" She rubbed her belly hopefully. "Name a price. Keep in mind that money is not a factor."

Gina smiled although she didn't like the woman upon hearing her proposal. The arrogance she presented by having access to her grandson's money angered her greatly. Instead she said, "Why darling, you had me at hello."

And so, the official invitation into Banks began.

Pending the birth of her biological great-grandsons, Ace and Walid, she was determined to not only remain in Banks' life, but also to protect all of them, including her biological great-granddaughter Minnesota Wales.

This was the sly behavior that caused Angie to hate her, but Gina felt her heart was in the right place.

How could she help Banks get further in life? Her answer came shortly after Banks, who was forced by Mason to choose between Jersey and his twin sons, was having a conversation with Jersey while Gina was in the room.

Banks said to Jersey, ***"Losing Bet made shit harder on the kids. All of 'em home now, even Joey. And they been asking questions on how she died. And I ain't got the answers to none of that shit. So, it's been fucking with my mind. Sometimes...sometimes I wish I could start all over, with just you and the boys."***

"Don't say that." Jersey said.

"I already did."

When Gina heard those words, like a genie in a bottle, she immediately got to work, starting with convincing Banks she could extend her help for the twins by moving into his home. All while he was on a visit at Jersey's estate.

"That's right, hold their heads like that," Gina said that day, showing Banks how to cradle two small babies at once. "And whatever you do, son, always remain calm when you hold infants this young. They absorb energy like sponges."

Hearing the advice, Banks took a deep breath and steadied himself. "You've been really good with my boys. Thank you."

Gina waved him off. "Don't worry. Your babies are such a pleasure it's almost like their taking care of me."

For some reason, Banks nodded and thought about the future. "I don't know what Mason has planned with Jersey, he, he's unpredictable. But if something happens to their mother, would you mind helping me take care of the boys?"

Out of his view she smiled sinisterly. "It'll be my pleasure."

Good luck came shortly after when Mason released Jersey to Banks but Gina, true to her word, became a fixture at the Wales' estate anyway.

But what about the wish that Banks made? To start all over with just him, Jersey and the twins.

She wanted to prove she was there for him and so she quickly came up with a plan. It was groundwork season.

The first thing she did was work on Banks while he was having a drink in his office at the Wales estate. Knocking on the door she said, "Mr. Wales, may I talk to you for a second?"

He nodded and sat his drink on his desk. "Sure, come in."

"I know I'm only here to take care of the twins but..." she looked down.

"What is it, Gina?" He frowned.

"I don't want to violate your sons trust. And I hope this can remain between us."

He grew serious and leaned forward. "I'm listening."

"Well, I overheard Spacey and Joey saying they feel that, well, since the arrival of the twins ..."

"Gina...just say it."

"This is hard, sir, but they feel you love your biological children more."

"What? How?"

"I don't know a lot but based on their words it's evident that they were referring to Minnesota and the twins. I haven't known you long, but I believe your love spreads to all of your children evenly. I just wish they felt that way too."

Banks stood up. "But I love all of them the same. Sure, over the past few months things have been crazy but...the love is always there."

"And I'm certain you're right. May I make a suggestion?"

"Yes."

"When the chance comes to prove it to the boys, maybe you should do whatever it takes."

With that seed planted in his mind, Gina intruded into Banks' life a little more. After all, her plan had many levels.

So, she continued her work, days later when Spacey was working out in the gym within the Wales estate. Gina walked in holding the babies. "There you are." Gina smiled.

Spacey frowned, wondering what the strange woman wanted as she touted around his brothers. Wiping his face with the towel he said, "Something wrong with them?" He grabbed Walid who stared him down as he held him in his arms.

"No, I, I was just thinking about something. I overheard you talking to Joey about your girlfriend not living up to your standards and, well, I think you should...never mind, maybe I'm imposing."

"No, tell me what you wanna say."

"May I make a suggestion?"

"Of course."

"A woman respects a man more who she must rely on."

He rocked Walid like he'd seen on TV, as if he was crying, but it was for nothing. The baby simply stared him down. "So, what should I do?"

"You're a wealthy man, who comes from money. Marry her and buy her a home. But put the title in only your name."

"Why would I do that?"

She shrugged and kissed Ace on the head when he cooed playfully. "She works?"

"Yes."

"Well a working woman will never submit to a man unless he's powerful. Powerful men get who and what they want. Always." She moved closer. "But you must own her. Make her your wife."

"Marry her?" He said, having never thought of it before.

"Yep, at the justice of the peace. In September. It's the month of love."

After digging into Spacey's head for the next week, he eventually proposed to her and purchased her home in full. And because Gina had already deposited the seeds of being available for his sons into Banks' mind, when Spacey said he would go to the justice of the peace, Banks demanded they marry in the home instead.

Which infuriated Minnesota beyond belief.

But still, Gina wasn't done.

One day Jersey was sitting in her room breastfeeding Ace. She already fed Walid and was gazing at Gina when she walked into the nursery.

"Hi," Jersey smiled. "Thank you for putting them on a schedule. It's done wonders for their sleep patterns."

"No problem." Gina smiled. "I just wish Banks was happier. He doesn't seem to be getting much rest. And is always deep in thought."

Jersey placed Ace in the baby swing with his brother. After securing him she tucked her breast away and walked up to her. "I don't, I don't understand. What's wrong with Banks?"

"I really hope we can keep this conversation between us."

"Sure, yes, anything you say will stay private."

Gina sighed. "Banks feels like Mason violated by involving himself into the twins' lives. He really wanted the moment with the babies to be about you and him."

"You know about that?"

"Of course, I do." She paused. "And I think you should do things over with him. The right way. So that the bond you two share will remain, beyond Mason."

"Wow. I didn't know he felt like that."

"May I make a suggestion?"

"Sure?"

"Give him another."

"Another baby?"

"Do you know a better way?"

After Gina spoke with Jersey, she was successfully able to convince her that they should have another child.

But again, Gina's work was not done.

Some moons later, Minnesota was eavesdropping on the phone conversation Tobias was having in his room when Gina walked up behind her. Embarrassed she was caught she thought it best to snap at the old woman. "What you doing walking up on me, bitch?"

"I'm sorry, I just overheard that your party is being cancelled."

Irritated all over again, Minnesota folded her arms and stormed down the hallway with Gina keeping up the pace. "Yeah, it's wrong."

"I agree."

Minnesota paused having gained and ally. "You do?"

"Yes. Very rude and disrespectful to your feelings. But may I make a suggestion?"

"Yes." She nodded rapidly.

"I think you should save your money and buy a place of your own."

"Why?"

"Because the best way to convince a parent that they need you, is by not needing them. Build your own future. Get your own apartment and then Banks will realize he misses you more."

The thought of moving out scared her to death. "I don't know about that."

"My dear, I'm older. Way older. Independence is the only way." She sighed deeply. "The good thing is you're the only daughter. As long as that doesn't change, you'll always have him eating out of your hands."

And so, Minnesota began spending more time out of the house, and Gina felt confident she was on her way yet again to making Banks' goal a realization. With no one living in the household outside of Banks, Jersey and their new family.

But there was one more person.

Joey Wales.

One evening Joey was sitting in his room playing video games when Gina walked inside. "What you doing in my room? You gotta knock first."

"Joey, I'm sorry, I just, I just wanted to come by and tell you that you shouldn't feel bad."

He frowned. "Bad for what?"

"Maybe I shouldn't say anything." She turned to walk away.

He dropped the controller by his foot and stood up. "Wait! What is it?"

She smiled, wiped the grin off her face and turned around. "If I tell you this, I'm gonna really need you to keep things between us."

He nodded. "O...okay."

"From what I overheard Spacey saying to Banks, it appeared that, well, people blame you for your mother's death. Saying that on the island you didn't care for her enough. Saying that if you had, she would be alive because Banks would not have divorced her."

Gina got this information from Minnesota's diary, but he didn't know. Instead, Joey immediately felt ill. Not because he was shocked but because she was reaffirming everything he believed in his heart.

His guilt was one of the main reasons he left the house for a little while when they returned from the island. Because when he was there, and Banks was gone, instead of giving his mother the mental attention she required, he was too busy having sex with Rosa's daughters. And so, he never got over the guilt.

"May I make a suggestion?"

"Sure." He said with a lowered head.

"Maybe you should leave. And give them some space. That's what I would do if I were in your position."

It was done.

A little while afterwards, Joey left the house and stayed with a girl who liked him from the jump. The problem was, time had gotten in the way and she also was into drugs. Before long, he adapted her habits quickly, eventually becoming an addict too.

Although not the plan, Gina didn't care about Joey's newfound issues. In her mind she successfully granted Banks' wishes.

But what about Mason Louisville?

Was it possible that her evilness reached to him too?

Before even coming to the Wales' home.

The answer is yes.

After discovering her grandson Banks Wales, earlier in the game, it didn't take her long to find out about his lifelong friend Mason. Gathering information from afar, it was clear that the two had a relationship that spanned many dark days. And that nothing could tear them apart.

Or could it?

She set out to see if she could destroy their bond. In her opinion he was bad news.

More leg work later, Gina was able to volunteer her time in the mental institution Mason was remanded after he tried to take his life, when his son Patterson was killed by his own brother. She decided to pay him a visit while he was loaded with drugs.

Armed with valuable information, about the pending plan for Jersey to give birth to Banks' child, she walked into his room wearing a nurse's uniform, with a different color wig of course.

On the first day he awakened, after Banks left from a visit, she was in his room next. "How are you feeling?"

He sat up in bed. "Who are you?"

"Consider me a friend."

High out of his mind, he rubbed his head. "Well what do you want?"

"To help."

"How the fuck you going to do that?"

"While you lying in this bed, your friend who has visited you every day since you've been out, is not only fucking your wife, but preparing to impregnate her as you sleep."

He laughed. "I won't even tell you how that's impossible."

Now she was the one laughing. "Let me make this clear. I am aware that Banks Wales was born as Blakeslee. And I'm aware that he's rich, having secured a successful career as a hood pharmacist. And I'm aware he's fucking Jersey."

Mason ran a hand down his face. "I knew, I knew about them."

She frowned. "So, you allowed this to go down?"

"I didn't think they were in love. I was hoping it would fizz out. My son told me they were together, and I had her followed when she left our house."

"You knew about the baby too?"

"No...this...this part is...this part hurts."

"Well now you are aware." She stepped closer to the bed. "If you don't fill this up, they will have a baby using a complete stranger's sperm." She removed a urine cup with a cap from her purse. "Shouldn't that father be you?"

After learning of his friend's baby deceit, Mason did give her his semen and she successfully paid a technician in the fertility clinic to exchange the donor they selected for Mason's sperm instead.

Her plan was to destroy their bond, by revealing Mason's betrayal. But once again, it backfired because it appeared that nothing could tear the friends apart.

But she had one plan left.

If she couldn't save Banks from himself, what about the twins Ace and Walid?

So, while the wedding ceremony went on downstairs, she successfully bundled the babies, and stole them away into the night.

CHAPTER TWENTY-FIVE
PRESENT DAY

Minnesota was driving down the road with Myrio in the passenger seat of the car he bought her. Tears were streaming down her face because although she had rejected Tobias, she held on to the hope that maybe they could possibly be together in the future.

He was something like an insurance policy.

And now the man was dead.

Had he fought for her a little more, she would have gladly accepted him back, but he seemed resigned to her distance.

"How long you gonna cry over dumb shit?" Myrio asked.

It had been less than an hour. But he put on as if years passed.

She sniffled and wiped her tears while also focusing on the road. "He was a good friend, Myrio. Stop being rude!"

"Nah, what he was, was Bolero's son."

She frowned. "How did you know that?"

"Everybody knows."

"So what? He was still nice! Right now, I don't even know what to do."

"I don't believe that. Your father has been distant. You said he doesn't respect you. Maybe he will respect you more if you gave him a reason."

"How?"

"Go directly to Bolero. Leverage what happened tonight for your future. Tell him about his son's death."

She finally understood. "And then what? Even if he put me on, I don't have any contacts with anybody on the streets. I don't even have enough money. Outside of the few dollars I was saving to get my own place."

"I can handle the details. All you have to do is decide what you wanna do. It's moments like this that separate the weak from the strong. So, tell me Minnesota, which one are you?"

Quincy Lipman and Laura laughed playfully in the back of a silver S Class Mercedes on the way to the Charles Street theater in Baltimore city. A friend of his was showing his documentary on the turn of politics in America.

Pretty boring shit.

But he was in the backseat getting chauffeured and freaky.

"Stick your finger deeper inside," Laura said as she whispered in his ear. "It feels so good."

The couple was drunk off wine and horny as fuck.

"What about him?" He asked looking at the driver.

"We're only using him for tonight," she shrugged. "Why should we care if he sees us? We'll never have to see him again."

"Laura," he shook his head as his finger tickled her clit. "I'm a well-known doctor." He kissed her cheek. "What if he recognizes us?"

She ruffled his blonde hair and covered her red hair over her face. "Now he can't see me." She joked.

He shook his head and suckled her bottom lip, as he pressed his fingers deeper into her pussy. When his dick hardened, he said, "Get on top."

She giggled. "What about the driver? Suddenly you don't care anymore?"

"Fuck him."

She laughed harder, sat on his lap, lifted her skirt and pushed over her panties. He quickly pressed into her wet pussy. Up and down she rose as if they were on a wave. "You feel so good, Quincy. And I'm gonna want more of this tonight."

"You can have as much as you need."

They continued about their fuck session until they realized the car had suddenly stopped. When Quincy turned his head to the left and looked out the window, he was shocked that they were parked on a dark road.

How did they get there?

Pushing Laura to the side like ugly clothes on a rack, he was shocked when he saw Preach aiming a phone camera their way in the driver's seat.

He shoved Laura again so hard, her head banged against the window. She rubbed the bruise. "Oww! Why did you—?"

"Who are you?" Quincy asked, tucking his dick into his pants.

Silence.

"Who are you?" He repeated.

Laura pulled down her dress and said, "Hey, he asked you a fucking—."

Her sentence was cut short when a bullet came piercing into the window and ripped through her skull. Blood splattered on the doctor's face in a mist.

When she was dead Preach unlocked the door, and his partner dragged her body to the ground.

Seeing the horror, Quincy pissed on himself.

About his business, Preach pushed the door open, walked to the doctor's side and grabbed him out.

From his view Quincy could see another car waiting some feet away.

Dusting the glass off Quincy's shoulders Preach said, "You disrespected a friend of mine not too long ago. Do you remember him?"

"I have no idea who you're talking about! But I'll have you know that I'm a very powerful man who—."

Preach slapped him. "Your white privilege doesn't matter here. Do you remember my friend or not?"

Trembling he said, "No, I have never..." suddenly he saw Banks' face in his mind and recalled his words. His blood ran cold. "I'm sorry, I, I mean, I had no experience in his, his—."

He slapped him again. "Shut up. The damage is done."

"What do you want with me," he wept quietly.

"You have entered the dark world. And in this world, there are rules. So, let me tell you what will happen next. You will come with me. No questions asked. Or I will make your life a living hell."

When he said that, two men walked out of the woods and a third stepped out of the parked car. "Why are you doing this?"

"You disrespected the wrong person. And for that you'll pay."

"What if I...what if I don't come?" He raised his chin, trying to put on that he was tougher than he was.

It didn't go over well.

"You just killed a woman."

Quincy pointed at himself. "Me, no I didn't! That was you!"

"Nah, that was you. People don't care about truth. They care about what you can prove. And what I can prove is this, you told your friend Davis that Laura was becoming a problem. Mainly because she wanted you to do things that were out of the possibility. Trips around the world. Why? Because you have a wife who is in the hospital right now fighting cancer. Now you also told this friend, you would do anything to have her disappear. We have the audio, trust me. They will buy my story."

"Wait a minute! I didn't pay anybody to—."

Preach slapped him again. "They will believe that you paid them, because she's dead. I mean think about it, you are fucking a twenty-year-old while your wife is dying in the hospital. Do you really wanna play who's the worst villain? Or do you want to get in that car over there?"

Quincy looked at the vehicle where the stranger stood, swallowed and walked toward the car.

Quincy, followed by Preach and three soldiers, walked into a large room inside Jersey's estate were Banks lie on a bed.

His eyes were closed. Mason was at his side in a panicked state and the moment he saw the doctor he rushed up to him. "Are you the head doctor?" He yelled.

He frowned. "I'm a neurologist." He walked up to Banks' bedside with authority. "What's wrong with her?" He looked at them.

"Him!" Mason glared. "And we don't know, nigga! You tell us!"

"Mason…" Preach said.

"Nah, you brought him here for a reason." He looked at Quincy. "Now save my fucking friend!"

Quincy removed his cell phone from his pocket. Raising his lid, he shined a light into Banks' left eye followed by the right. Turning the light off he shook his head.

"What is it?" Mason asked.

"His right pupil isn't responding to light and the optic nerve is discolored."

Mason stepped back. "What…what that mean?"

"It's a sign that can indicate a growth of some sort."

"Why a different color?" Spacey asked.

"A tumor if large enough, can press against the back of the optic nerve. Making it pale."

Once the calm one, upon hearing the news Preach stepped up. "Then what you gonna do? Because this man can't die."

"Well then we need to get him to a hospital."

"No hospitals!" Mason yelled. "Banks made that clear."

Quincy frowned. "But I'm not equipped to handle this alone. We need—"

"Do I have to remind you about red head?" Preach asked referring to his dead girlfriend. "Now we can get whatever equipment you need in this room. But he stays here."

He looked around from where he stood. It was obvious the location would have to do. "This room will have to be completely sterilized and I'll need a lot of powerful equipment and a crew."

"Whatever you need you got." Mason said.

"Don't be too excited. The procedure is risky. And if this man dies it'll be on your heads." Quincy said arrogantly.

"You wanna say that shit to me again?" Mason asked.

"No, my, my apologies." He sighed and looked at his phone. "Let me make a few calls."

Mason tapped Preach and they walked across the room. "Where are the twins?" He whispered.

"We have a crew out right now looking. But I'm pretty sure they're with Gina."

"What the fuck does she want from us?"

"She's definitely Banks' grandmother. We have her daughter Carmen and it's been verified. Apparently, she's been following Banks for years. And from what I heard she was the one who, well, came into your room and took your sperm for..."

Mason took two steps back. "I always thought she looked familiar but...I mean...I couldn't place her face."

"From what I'm told she wants a relationship with her biological family. That includes the twins, Banks and Minnesota."

"Wait, she has her too?"

"No, at least we don't think so."

Mason dragged a hand down his face. "This the last thing we need right now."

"Facts. The problem is this woman is very rich and has a lot of pull. She's also very calculating and motivated. They are her family. She can move in ways we won't see coming."

"And what about Bolero? He can't find out about Tobias."

Preach nodded. "I know. Right now, he's at a suite with his daughters. When Banks was escorted out the house, we had our men close down the celebrations early. But from what I'm hearing, Cassandra keeps asking about Tobias. I don't know how much longer we'll be able to hold him off. It could mean war."

Mason turned around and looked at Banks lying on the bed. "Right now, nothing matters more to me than Banks. He can't die on me. We left too much unsaid."

WANT TO DISCUSS?

JOIN OUR FACEBOOK GROUP:

T. STYLES' 'WAR SAGA" READING GROUP

The Cartel Publications Order Form

www.thecartelpublications.com

Inmates **ONLY** receive novels for $10.00 per book **PLUS** shipping fee **PER BOOK.**

(Mail Order **MUST** come from inmate directly to receive discount)

Shyt List 1	________	$15.00
Shyt List 2	________	$15.00
Shyt List 3	________	$15.00
Shyt List 4	________	$15.00
Shyt List 5	________	$15.00
Shyt List 6	________	$15.00
Pitbulls In A Skirt	________	$15.00
Pitbulls In A Skirt 2	________	$15.00
Pitbulls In A Skirt 3	________	$15.00
Pitbulls In A Skirt 4	________	$15.00
Pitbulls In A Skirt 5	________	$15.00
Victoria's Secret	________	$15.00
Poison 1	________	$15.00
Poison 2	________	$15.00
Hell Razor Honeys	________	$15.00
Hell Razor Honeys 2	________	$15.00
A Hustler's Son	________	$15.00
A Hustler's Son 2	________	$15.00
Black and Ugly	________	$15.00
Black and Ugly As Ever	________	$15.00
Ms Wayne & The Queens of DC **(LGBT)**	________	$15.00
Black And The Ugliest	________	$15.00
Year Of The Crackmom	________	$15.00
Deadheads	________	$15.00
The Face That Launched A Thousand Bullets	________	$15.00
The Unusual Suspects	________	$15.00
Paid In Blood	________	$15.00
Raunchy	________	$15.00
Raunchy 2	________	$15.00
Raunchy 3	________	$15.00
Mad Maxxx (4th Book Raunchy Series)	________	$15.00
Quita's Dayscare Center	________	$15.00
Quita's Dayscare Center 2	________	$15.00
Pretty Kings	________	$15.00
Pretty Kings 2	________	$15.00
Pretty Kings 3	________	$15.00
Pretty Kings 4	________	$15.00
Silence Of The Nine	________	$15.00
Silence Of The Nine 2	________	$15.00
Silence Of The Nine 3	________	$15.00
Prison Throne	________	$15.00

Drunk & Hot Girls	________	$15.00
Hersband Material **(LGBT)**	________	$15.00
The End: How To Write A Bestselling Novel In 30 Days (Non-Fiction Guide)	________	$15.00
Upscale Kittens	________	$15.00
Wake & Bake Boys	________	$15.00
Young & Dumb	________	$15.00
Young & Dumb 2: Vyce's Getback	________	$15.00
Tranny 911 **(LGBT)**	________	$15.00
Tranny 911: Dixie's Rise **(LGBT)**	________	$15.00
First Comes Love, Then Comes Murder	________	$15.00
Luxury Tax	________	$15.00
The Lying King	________	$15.00
Crazy Kind Of Love	________	$15.00
Goon	________	$15.00
And They Call Me God	________	$15.00
The Ungrateful Bastards	________	$15.00
Lipstick Dom **(LGBT)**	________	$15.00
A School of Dolls **(LGBT)**	________	$15.00
Hoetic Justice	________	$15.00
KALI: Raunchy Relived (5th Book in Raunchy Series)	________	$15.00
Skeezers	________	$15.00
Skeezers 2	________	$15.00
You Kissed Me, Now I Own You	________	$15.00
Nefarious	________	$15.00
Redbone 3: The Rise of The Fold	________	$15.00
The Fold (4th Redbone Book)	________	$15.00
Clown Niggas	________	$15.00
The One You Shouldn't Trust	________	$15.00
The WHORE The Wind Blew My Way	________	$15.00
She Brings The Worst Kind	________	$15.00
The House That Crack Built	________	$15.00
The House That Crack Built 2	________	$15.00
The House That Crack Built 3	________	$15.00
The House That Crack Built 4	________	$15.00
Level Up **(LGBT)**	________	$15.00
Villains: It's Savage Season	________	$15.00
Gay For My Bae	________	$15.00
War	________	$15.00
War 2: All Hell Breaks Loose	________	$15.00
War 3: The Land Of The Lou's	________	$15.00
War 4: Skull Island	________	$15.00
War 5: Karma	________	$15.00
War 6: Envy	________	$15.00

(**Redbone 1** & **2** are **NOT** Cartel Publications novels and if **ordered** the cost is **FULL** price of $15.00 **each**. **No Exceptions**.)

Please add **$5.00** for shipping and handling fees for up to **(2) BOOKS PER ORDER**.

Inmates too!

(See Next Page for ORDER DETAILS)

The Cartel Publications * P.O. BOX 486 OWINGS MILLS MD 21117

Name: ______________________________

Address: ______________________________

City/State: ______________________________

Contact/Email: ______________________________

Please allow 8-10 BUSINESS days Before shipping.

The Cartel Publications is NOT responsible for Prison Orders rejected!

NO RETURNS and NO REFUNDS
NO PERSONAL CHECKS ACCEPTED
STAMPS NO LONGER ACCEPTED

Made in the USA
Monee, IL
30 January 2020